# CITY OF THE DEAD

# CITY OF THE DEAD

*The Third Egyptian Mystery*

## ANTON GILL

## BLOOMSBURY

First published in Great Britain 1993

Copyright © 1993 by Anton Gill

The moral right of the author has been asserted

Bloomsbury Publishing Ltd, 2 Soho Square, London W1V 5DE

A CIP catalogue record for this book is available from the British Library

ISBN 0 7475 1486 0

10 9 8 7 6 5 4 3 2 1

Typeset by Hewer Text Composition Services, Edinburgh
Printed in Great Britain by Clays Ltd, St Ives PLC

for Joe Steeples

## AUTHOR'S NOTE

The historical background to the story which follows is broadly correct, but the majority of the characters are fictional. We know a good deal about ancient Egypt because its inhabitants were highly developed, literate, and had a sense of history; even so, experts estimate that in the 200 years since the science of Egyptology began, only twenty-five per cent of what could be known has been revealed, and there is still much disagreement about certain dates and events amongst scholars. However, I do apologise to Egyptologists and purists, who may read this and take exception to such unscholarly conduct, for the occasional freedoms I have allowed myself.

# THE BACKGROUND TO HUY'S EGYPT

The nine years of the reign of the young pharaoh Tutankhamun, 1361–1352 B C, were troubled ones for Egypt. They came at the end of the Eighteenth Dynasty, the most glorious of all the thirty dynasties of the empire. Tutankhamun's predecessors had been mainly illustrious warrior kings, who created a new empire and consolidated the old; but just before him a strange, visionary pharaoh had occupied the throne: Akhenaten. He had thrown out all the old gods and replaced them with one, the Aten, who had his being in the life-giving sunlight. Akhenaten was the world's first recorded philosopher and the inventor of monotheism. In the seventeen years of his reign he made enormous changes in the way his country thought and was run; but in the process he lost the whole of the northern empire (modern Palestine and Syria), and brought the country to the brink of ruin. Now, powerful enemies were thronging on the northern and eastern frontiers.

Akhenaten's religious reforms had driven doubt into the minds of his people after generations of unchanged certainty which went back to before the building of the pyramids one thousand years earlier, and although the empire itself, already over 1,500 years old at the time of these stories, had been through bad times before, Egypt now entered a short dark age. Akhenaten had not been popular with the priest-administrators of the old religion, whose power he took away, or with ordinary people, who saw him as a defiler of their long-held beliefs, especially in the afterlife and the dead. Since his death in 1362 B C, the new capital city he had built for himself (Akhetaten

– the City of the Horizon), quickly fell into ruin as power reverted to Thebes (the Southern Capital; the northern seat of government was at Memphis). Akhenaten's name was cut from every monument, and people were not even allowed to speak it.

Akhenaten died without a direct heir, and the short reigns of the three kings who succeeded him, of which Tutankhamun's was the second and by far the longest, were fraught with uncertainty. During this time the pharaohs themselves had their power curbed and controlled by Horemheb, formerly Commander-in-Chief of Akhenaten's army, but now bent on fulfilling his own ambition to restore the empire and the old religion, and to become pharaoh himself – he did so finally in 1348 BC and reigned for twenty-eight years, the last king of the Eighteenth Dynasty, marrying Akhenaten's sister-in-law to reinforce his claim to the throne.

Egypt was to rally under Horemheb and early in the Nineteenth Dynasty it achieved one last glorious peak under Rameses II. It was by far the most powerful and the wealthiest country in the known world, rich in gold, copper and precious stones. Trade was carried out the length of the Nile from the coast to Nubia, and on the Mediterranean (the Great Green), and the Red Sea as far as Punt (Somaliland). But it was a narrow strip of a country, clinging to the banks of the Nile and hemmed in to the east and west by deserts, and governed by three seasons: spring, *shemu*, was the time of drought, from February to May; summer, *akhet*, was the time of the Nile flood, from June to October; and autumn, *peret*, was the time of coming forth, when the crops grew. The ancient Egyptians lived closer to the seasons than we do. They also believed that the heart was the centre of thought.

The decade in which the stories take place – a minute period of ancient Egypt's 3,000-year history – was nevertheless a crucial one for the country. It was becoming aware of the world beyond its frontiers, and of the possibility that it, too, might one day be conquered and come to an end. It was a time of uncertainty, questioning, intrigue and violence. A distant mirror in which we can see something of ourselves.

The ancient Egyptians worshipped a great number of gods. Some of them were restricted to cities or localities, while others waxed and waned in importance with time. Certain gods were duplications of the same 'idea'. Here are some of the most important, as they appear in the stories:

AMUN  The chief god of the Southern Capital, Thebes. Represented as a man, and associated with the supreme sun god, Ra. Animals dedicated to him were the ram and the goose.

ANUBIS  The jackal god of embalming.

ATEN  The god of the sun's energy, represented as the sun's disc whose rays end in protecting hands.

BES  A dwarf god, part lion. Protector of the hearth.

GEB  The earth god, represented as a man.

HAPY  The god of the Nile.

HATHOR The cow goddess; the suckler of the king.

HORUS  The hawk god, son of Osiris and Isis, and therefore a member of the most important trinity in ancient Egyptian theology.

ISIS  The divine mother.

KHONS  The god of the moon; son of Amun.

MAAT  The goddess of truth.

MIN  The god of human fertility.

MUT  Wife of Amun, originally a vulture goddess. The vulture was the animal of Upper (southern) Egypt. Lower (northern) Egypt was represented by the cobra.

OSIRIS  The god of the underworld. The afterlife was of central importance to the thinking of the Ancient Egyptians.

RA  The great god of the sun.

SET  The god of storms and violence; brother and murderer of Osiris. Very roughtly equivalent to Satan.

SOBEK  The crocodile god.

THOTH  The ibis-headed god of writing. His associated animal was the baboon.

# PRINCIPAL CHARACTERS OF *CITY OF THE DEAD*

(in order of appearance)

Fictional characters are in capitals, historical characters in lower case.

Tutankhamun: Pharaoh, 1361–1352 BC
Ay: His wife's grandfather. Co-regent
Akhenaten: The disgraced recent predecessor of Tutankhamun, now known as the Great Criminal
Horemheb: Co-regent with Ay and rival to the succession
Ankhsenpaamun (Ankhsi): Tutankhamun's Great Wife
Tey: Ay's Chief Wife
Nezemmut: Horemheb's wife
HUY: Former scribe
TAHEB: Shipowner. Widow and heiress of Huy's friend Amotju
KENAMUN: Police chief. Former priest-administrator in the Southern Capital
AHMOSE: Courtier
NEHESY: Chief huntsman
SHERYBIN: Charioteer
INENY: Ay's secretary
Zannanzash: Hittite prince
MERINAKHTE: Doctor
HORAHA: Chief doctor
SENSENEB: His daughter
HAPU: His steward
AAHETEP: Nehesy's wife
NUBENEHEM: Brothel keeper

# ONE

The king bit his lip. The interview had gone badly. He watched the general's retreating back with murder in his heart. How much longer would he have to put up with the curbs of this ambitious old man?

To begin with, he had been grateful for Horemheb's experience, and he had leant on him. But it was four floods since his coronation, and at seventeen years old, he was still pharaoh in name only. The army, his spies told him, remained loyal to Horemheb, its commander since the days of his predecessor, the disgraced pharaoh Akhenaten. He would have to work on getting them to transfer their loyalty to him. Then he would see about sending Horemheb off on a diplomatic mission to some remote province. He toyed with the idea of assassination, but knew that the day when he felt secure enough to have that done was still far off.

Then there was Ay, even older, but just as ambitious, and as much of a thorn in his side. The king was well aware that both these men – joint regents in doubtful alliance during his minority – wanted only one thing – to wear the *pschent* themselves. He made a point of having the red-and-white double crown of the Black Land placed on his head at every meeting with his two advisers, as they now liked to be called, though down the years General Horemheb, the stronger of the two, had got the young king to confer a greater string of titles on him than any commoner had ever carried in the entire history of the country, and that stretched back through one and a half recorded millennia, and eighteen dynasties.

Ay had been Akhenaten's father-in-law. Another commoner. The son of a Mitannite whose sister had the good fortune to become Great Wife of Menkheprure Tuthmosis, grandfather of Akhenaten, he had put it about – and the pharaoh could not disprove it – that he was also the brother of Tiy, Akhenaten's mother. Ay had further consolidated his position in the royal household by marrying off his daughter Nefertiti to Akhenaten. The girl, the most beautiful ever seen in the Black Land, became the king's Great Wife, by whom he produced seven daughters. The present king was married to the third daughter, who had much of her mother's beauty. But the family net Ay had woven around the young pharaoh had not endeared him.

'I am king. Nebkheprure Tutankhamun.' He said his name to himself as the high steward removed the heavy crown and replaced it with a blue-and-gold headdress – lapis and gold leaf over a light leather frame. The king sniffed the leather, enjoying the smell. His name gave him confidence. He wanted it on the people's lips, on columns, pylons, temples and city gates. He would be the redeemer of the country, the man who would bring the Black Land back its glory after the sombre years of failure and doubt which had preceded his reign. But, he thought angrily, returning to his original theme, to be entered as such a king in the papyri of the scribes of history, he would first have to emerge from the shadows of his 'advisers'. And, if he was to found a dynasty that would sweep aside all remaining doubts about his own remote legitimacy of descent, and therefore his own claim to the throne, he must have a son. So far, in the five years of marriage that had passed since Ankhsenpaamun grew capable of motherhood and they had started to share a bed, they had not even been able to produce a girl. He had no doubt of his own powers – he had two sons and three daughters by concubines already – but their claim to lineage was not strong enough, and he had no illusions about their chance of survival if he were not there to protect them against the cunning Ay and the predatory Horemheb.

How could two old men thwart him like this? Horemheb

was all of fifty-five, and Ay ten years more than that. Yet they were as thirsty for power as men half their age. The king supposed that the lust stemmed from years of frustration, but their ability to survive was borne out by the fact that after the fall of Akhenaten they had emerged not only with their careers intact but in key positions of power which they had immediately and ruthlessly consolidated. Tutankhamun himself was in no doubt at all that they had brought about the fall and the death of the old king, though even to consider killing the pharaoh was on a level of blasphemy to start the demons of Set howling.

He made himself calm down. What was needed above all to combat these two was a clear head. He had few friends and they were all his age or younger. Inspecting the stables a few days earlier, where he was showing off his new Assyrian hunting horses to a group of young barons, he had been surprised by a visit from Horemheb, who, with his usual mock servility, had requested a meeting. Horemheb had not come alone into the presence of his king, but had the arrogance, then as always, to arrive flanked by half a dozen of his special Medjays. Tutankhamun had felt like the leader of a schoolboy gang surprised raiding date palms by the farmer. The memory irritated him to such an extent that even now he clenched his teeth and balled his fists, as he wished the general a violent death. *Tear out his eyes*! But as soon as the image was past, Tutankhamun cursed himself for not being able to maintain his decision for even a moment to keep cool blood.

Snapping his fingers for wine, he told the major domo that he wished to be washed and made-up afresh. The interview with Horemheb had unsettled him, and it had come hard on the heels of new information from his spies which had been even more perturbing. They had revealed a plan of Ay's – though nothing could be substantiated – to marry Ankhsenpaamun, if anything should happen to him.

He knew that this was merely a political contingency plan: marrying the dead king's wife would strengthen his successor's claim. Ay already had a Chief Wife, Tey, Nefertiti's stepmother, to whom he had been married for as long as anyone could remember, and to whom he appeared to be devoted. But the thought that Ay could contemplate outliving him disturbed Tutankhamun; and as for the idea of Ankhsi having to go to bed with a man fifty years her senior, it was too disgusting to contemplate. The king wished that he were ten years older himself. Then he would be able to outmanoeuvre these two crocodiles who had been experienced sons of guile before the Eight Elements which formed him had joined in his mother's birth-cave.

He told himself that Ay's plan would come to nothing. He had even half begun to devise a plan to neutralise Ay by spreading a rumour in Horemheb's camp that the old Master of Horse was plotting against him. He was doubtful of its success. Horemheb appeared to need Ay to balance his own power game; just as the little crabs that scuttled in and out of their holes along the bank of the river held up an enormous claw and a minute one.

It was not outside the bounds of possibility that Horemheb would use Ay to catch him in a pincer movement, thought the king, as the little crabs scuttled out of his heart to give way to consideration of the meeting he had just had with the general. Anger bubbled up again as he remembered that Horemheb had turned his back before leaving the audience chamber; but Tutankhamun managed to control it this time.

Horemheb had come alone, for once. His proposal had been outrageous. The king had requested – requested of a subject! – time to consider, but in reality he knew that there was little he could do to prevent it. The general wanted to marry Nezemmut.

The pincer movement again. For a moment of panic, the king saw himself outmanoeuvred on the *senet* board, saw himself dispensed with before he had begun to reign. Nezemmut was now twenty-four. She had never had quite the beauty of her older sister Nefertiti, but she had a far more durable character, and she had ridden out the storm following the fall

4

of Akhenaten without recourse to her father's protection. She had a dark, strong face, her eyes full of sexual challenge and threat. If Nefertiti's looks reminded you of the sky, Nezemmut's made you think of the earth.

She had been married to a son of the Hittite king Selpel, but the marriage was annulled after the Hittites withdrew their friendship from the Black Land. Since then, she had lived in the palace at the City of the Horizon, and her affair with the sensitive picture painter, Auta, was an open secret mildly disapproved of by the king. With the collapse of the city, Tutankhamun had brought her back with him to the Southern Capital as part of his retinue – and, as he now remembered with another little stab of irritation, at Horemheb's suggestion.

How deeply laid were the general's plans? And how patient was he? The king could see immediately that a marriage to Nezemmut would strengthen a future claim to the throne by Horemheb. The girl would be preferable to any of Akhenaten's surviving daughters – the younger ones were now at marrying age – because the stigma of being related by blood to the Great Criminal did not attach to her. As body servants brought water in a golden bowl and washed his face and arms, the king's thoughts turned uneasily to his own connivance at the blacking of Akhenaten's name. It had been necessary to underpin his own legitimacy as pharaoh; and of course the campaign had been planned, engineered and executed by Horemheb, riding roughshod over Ay's weak objections at the vilification of his former son-in-law. At the time, Tutankhamun had believed that Horemheb was simply helping him; giving the line of succession the sort of boost it needed after so much chaos and uncertainty. Now, looking back, it seemed to the king that Horemheb had been helping himself. He appeared to be nothing but another one of the general's tools. As long as he accepted that role he would be safe for as long as the general chose; but if he resisted . . .

Tutankhamun drew himself up. If he resisted, he had better be perfectly sure of success.

He watched the girl mixing make-up from a cake with water and a linen pad. She approached, avoiding eye contact, which was forbidden to all but the highest servants. He would have to lay plans even deeper than the general's, and he would have to strike hard and accurately, and only when he was absolutely sure that the blow would be fatal. In the meantime, he would redouble his efforts to get a child. He would have Ankhsi secretly examined, and he would pray with her to Renenutet and Tawaret, Hathor and Bes. If there could be a boy child, he would show him to the army. He would assume command – his royal right – before Horemheb could object.

As the girl dabbed on the make-up, he sensed her breath on his cheek. He felt better. A glow began inside him, and he raised his head. He would permit this marriage to Nezemmut. It could always be broken off later, and if Horemheb had children they would die with their father as soon as the king was strong enough. His heart dwelt on that day and his thoughts were glad.

# TWO

Everyone had something to gain, thought Ay as he watched his younger daughter take the hand of Horemheb and exchange vows with him. The usually simple ceremony had been blown up into a state occasion by the general, who had secured the king's permission to hold it in the temple of Amun.

Ay was not sure about the young pharaoh's recent acquiescence to Horemheb's requests. He had been sure that Tutankhamun was on the point of rebelling against them, and had told Horemheb so during one of their infrequent meetings, following the hearing of the reports of the viziers of the north and south. Horemheb had laughed at the idea, but Ay was left with the impression of being excluded, and since then had seen a scorpion under every stone.

He wrung his hands as he held them in front of him, and his heavy rings scraped against one another. The assembly stood in a long, pillared hall, the priests at one end by the *naos*, in white robes and multicoloured headdresses; the nobles were ranged along the sides and squeezed between the pillars. His gaze travelled upwards to the painted lotus flowers of their capitals. Ay read the inscriptions carved into them, and noticed where the names of the disgraced had been cut out. In some places he could see where his own name had been inserted, squeezed in to give credence to his lineage. He wondered how long his cartouches would stand. Everywhere he took care that he was represented as a young and vigorous man, and he promoted an image of himself as one whose personality and years combined strength with wisdom and experience. But he was fighting a losing battle against the patient, raw energy of Horemheb's ambition, and he knew it.

He glanced across to the dais where the king and queen sat with their retinue, a splash of pale blues, golds and greens among the white robes and kilts most of the others wore. It was too far away for Ay to be able to see the king's expression, but the proud, cold bearing of the body was scarcely expressive of joy.

As for the couple, whose voices rose to the high roof and rebounded back down to the throng from the massive stone cross-blocks and heavy cedar roof-planks, their faces betrayed little. Nezemmut might have been wearing a mask, and Horemheb's huge, battered head bore such a network of deep wrinkles that no one expression could be deduced from their juxtaposition. The brown eyes shone within that tanned sea of crevices but knew how to keep their secrets, showing no more than alert and undiminished intelligence. Horemheb, it was said, could deal with five problems simultaneously in his heart.

The sun, descending on his journey west, suddenly slipped his light through the tall, narrow entrance of the temple and spread his wings within, darting rays here and there, dancing on the cream and red, blue and gold of the columns and walls. As if Ra himself had sent the signal, the musicians struck up the sistra and the clappers, cymbals and bells. The king turned his head towards the light and now Ay could clearly discern the hard line of his mouth. If Horemheb had noticed it too he gave no sign. Outside, the people were calling his name as well as the pharaoh's. No one would deny what Horemheb had done for the Black Land, thought Ay; but perhaps there was also such a thing as too much gratitude.

Led by the king and his retinue, immediately succeeded by the newlyweds, the people in the temple filed out into the sunshine. It was still early in the season of *shemu*, and even at midday the heat was tolerable. Many of the noblewomen wore shawls of light wool over their pleated robes. The procession passed along the avenue which connected the temple to the main north-to-south axis road of the Southern Capital, where canopied litters awaited the greater among them. The music continued to play, and as the lesser guests arranged themselves in a loose order behind the litters for the walk to the palace compound and the three-day feast which would begin in an hour's time in the great shaded courtyard of Horemheb's house, a murmur of conversation was added to the sound of the instruments. The crowd lining the route waved palm fronds and cheered, throwing boughs under the feet of the robust copper-coloured men in kilts of dazzling white linen trimmed with gold who carried the litters of the king and queen, Horemheb, Nezemmut, and Ay. Behind the litter of the general's new wife danced her constant companions, the girl-dwarfs Para and Reneneh.

Amongst the protagonists of the celebration there was the least joy. Only a few perfunctory words had been exchanged between them as they entered their litters.

They would have to put on a better act than that at the feast, thought the former scribe, Huy, watching from a position near the front of the crowd. He saw the closed expressions of Horemheb and Nezemmut. Tutankhamun wore the impenetrable, ambivalent, mask-like look which he had developed during the last years of his adolescence. He might have been smiling inwardly, but there was no way you could be sure. His wife and Ay were the only ones whose faces could be read. Ankhsenpaamun looked worried. Ay seemed troubled, envious; but there was determination in the set of his thin-lipped, old man's mouth. For a moment the eyes of the former scribe and the former Master of Horse, both veterans of the disgraced Akhenaten's court, met. Was there a spark of recognition there, or was it just imagined? It was many years since they had last seen each other, and yet in the time that Huy had been back in the Southern Capital, forbidden to practise his former profession, he had built up a reputation as a problem solver. Aware of Horemheb's dislike of less powerful

9

fellow-adherents of the former regime, Huy had kept his head down, but could do nothing about the reputation he had won, due to which he was able to scrape a precarious living.

Lurking at the edges of the crowd, men from Horemheb's special section of Medjay police were not troubling to make their presence less than obvious. The general was flaunting his private power more and more flagrantly, but Huy was not sure why. Did he seek to prove to the king that he was the real power in the land? Or did he deliberately seek a confrontation with the young pharaoh? Despite all his sophistication, all the political dexterity he had learnt down the years, might it not perhaps be a case of an old lion showing his teeth to a young one – even though he knows that, once he has entered the *seqtet* boat, his power is doomed, and not even the flexing of all his muscles will pull him backwards one second in time?

Huy wondered if Horemheb was, after all, either subtle enough or modest enough ever to entertain such thoughts in his heart. The general was a practical man. Abstractions did not interest him, though he did make a show of an interest in the arts, pouring money into the hands of painters and carvers, singers and potters; imitating the manner of his own hero, the warrior pharaoh Menkheperre Tuthmosis, creator of the Great Empire, whose death a century earlier was still lamented, as from it the historians now dated the decline of power in the Black Land. Horemheb, Huy was certain, wanted to be the man to arrest that decline. Huy privately had little doubt that he would succeed, but he reserved a scrap of judgement because he remembered, years ago, a light of independence – or even of defiance – in the eyes of the young pharaoh, then only nine years old, as he fulfilled the rite of the Opening of the Mouth at the entombment of his immediate predecessor, Smenkhkare. Since then his every step, his every move, had been dogged by his two adviser-jailers. Huy wondered if, with maturity, the young king might not find the strength and the cunning to break the bars, shoot the bolts of the doors.

The litters had lumbered past him now, their bearers kicking up dust. Huy watched the swinging curtains and tried to imagine the private thoughts of the occupants of each. He doubted if the paymasters of the banquets to follow would enjoy them much. For a few minutes longer he watched the excited, chattering crowd of lesser guests and officials pass by, the headdresses glittering in the sun, a swirl of white linen and brown bodies whose precise outlines were softened by the fine dust their footsteps raised from the road. Huy's eyes sought Taheb among them. For a moment he thought he saw her, but he could not be sure, and something in his heart prevented him from looking further. It had been two years since their love bond had ended, after several false stops and starts. In that time he had seen her once, and then only at a distance, but it was enough to tell his heart that he had not forgotten her. Now here he was, hopelessly looking for her again. He knew he was chasing a dream, but the spectre remained. Exhausted by it, he sometimes wondered what it would take to lay this ghost.

He turned away from the procession, and shouldered his way through the press of people who lingered to watch until the last of the marriage guests had passed by. He felt at once disappointed at not pursuing Taheb, and relieved. If he were to meet her, he would have no words to say to her. Why, then, play with the illusion that they might be together again? As a palliative for loneliness? He knew in his heart that he did not want her back; if the desire had truly been there, he would have done something about it long ago.

Leaving the crowd behind him, the music growing fainter as he walked down the low hill on which the temple stood, he made his way home. For some time he had lived in a small house in the harbour quarter. A handful of years earlier, it had been bought for him by Ipuky, the Controller of the Silver Mines, and a man to whom he had been able to be of service. As a result of the work he had done at that time, a corrupt chief scribe had been exposed, and a vile brothel was closed; but although Ipuky, an official of high enough rank to have the ear of Horemheb, had interceded for him,

11

credit for the investigation had gone to the priest-administrator officially in charge, Kenamun. That had rankled with Huy. He knew that Kenamun himself had murdered a Babylonian prostitute, but the priest-administrator's rank had protected him from accusation, and Huy had had to accept defeat, taking consolation in the fact that public praise for him might have attracted unwelcome attention from Horemheb. Being human, however, it had been some time before he ceased to wish both men thrown to the crocodiles.

She awoke, immediately aware that her husband was already conscious, lying there in the darkness, staring at nothing, troubled by thoughts he only grudgingly shared with her, but which she found easy to guess. It was the lack of a child that kept him from sleep.

She sighed as softly as she could, so as not to let him know that she was awake, but she felt tension run through his muscles and knew that she had not kept her secret. He did not speak to her however, and for a long time they lay in silence, listening to the muffled island of sound that came from the feast in Horemheb's house on the other side of the palace compound. It had been a long day and she was tired – tired from the heavy regalia, and tired from the rich food and the wine.

In the darkness his hand found hers and grasped it. She curled her fingers gratefully round his, but did not know whether this affection proceeded from his heart or just from kindness. She was jealous of all that he kept back from her. She hated her body. Why would it not produce a child that lived? Only six months had passed since Horemheb's marriage, and now they were celebrating her aunt's pregnancy. Nezemmut, so much older than she, had peopled her birth-cave with no effort. Of what value, then, had their own six months of prayer and sacrifice to the gods of fertility been? Were the gods as stony as their images?

His hand moved up to her face and she turned it away so that he could not feel the tears on her cheeks. Perhaps her birth-cave was as barren as the City of the Horizon where she had been born: a city of the dead.

'It will be all right,' came the king's voice. He spoke with a gentleness that surprised her. 'The gods are leading Horemheb on in order to destroy him. As for the child that is coming to him, it will never sit on the Golden Chair.'

'I want you to be sure. I want you to have a direct heir.'

He put an arm round her. 'I will. We will.'

'Why do the gods not hear us? You are one of them. Or can Horemheb order them about as he does everyone else?'

Tutankhamun fought down anger at her remark, telling himself that he had to indulge the candour of someone who was, after all, not much more than a child.

'His days of giving orders are all but over.'

'And Ay?' she asked, not forgetting the other enemy.

'He is already out of the game.'

Ankhsenpaamun did not make any comment. She did not agree with her husband, but did not know why, and so decided to keep her silence. The king stroked her brow gently, wishing that tiredness and the nagging interruption of his thoughts were not preventing him from showing even the pretence of desire. He turned his heart to the plans that he had begun to lay secretly, not telling anyone except the few trusted men of his household who would carry them out. He did not feel that everything could be confidently left to the gods to sort out. In any case, he had to do something, and, unfocused as his plans were, it comforted him to consider them as they began to develop.

He soothed her back to sleep, thinking how young she was. Little Ankhsi, with her slim arms and her little breasts that barely showed. Would she ever grow into the strong, voluptuous woman her aunt had become? She seemed to the king like a flower on the point of opening.

Tutankhamun did not return to sleep so easily himself, though the regular breathing of his wife, its faint breeze on his chest, soothed him in turn. He had awakened from a dream

13

of hunting. The sand had been hard under the wheels of his lightest chariot, drawn by his two favourite horses from the north. They responded to the slightest touch, and the chariot was manoeuvrable enough to pursue the swiftest prey. Even the long spotted cat, the fastest animal, could not escape him.

In his dream he had been hunting the great birds, which had thundered ahead of him on their powerful legs, running in desperation and darting their idiotic heads on long naked necks hither and thither in panic. He wanted to make two kills, to collect enough black body feathers and white tail feathers for the golden flywhisks he had commissioned for the commemoration day of his queen's coming-forth. It was a point of honour to collect the feathers himself, and he was an experienced hunter. After the enforced inactivity of the court, hunting was his chief joy.

Now, he flew across the Western Desert near Kharga, it seemed; far, far out among the dunes and nowhere near his usual hunting grounds. The big black-and-white birds galloped directly ahead of the chariot, making half-hearted feints to right and left, but unable to manoeuvre their bulk out of harm's way. All he had to do was select his target and bring it down with his first harpoon. Then, a second target with the second weapon, and it would be over. They would return to the kills and his charioteer would take what they needed from the bodies, leaving the rest for the children of Nekhbet.

In his dream he wanted to pass the reins of the chariot over, to grasp the harpoon. It was only then that he realised he was alone. And now his horses were slowing, tiring, and the birds were making distance between them, running on into the desert in their flailing, grotesque way, until they became shimmering untidy specks in the heat, melting into the air, finally disappearing altogether, leaving him alone. The chariot came to a halt, and his beautiful dun horses, Hyksos-trained, so he had been told, sank under the sand. The chariot tilted forward on to its shaft and he had to grasp the side to steady himself.

14

The jolt had awakened him. At first he was relieved that it had been a dream, for it had seemed real enough, and his last dreaming thoughts had been despairing ones of leaving the empire without an heir to the mercy of Horemheb. Then he recognised where he was, heard his wife's gentle breathing, and knew, with a stab of irritation of which he felt ashamed, that before another minute had elapsed she would sense him awake and come back from sleep herself.

He looked at his Great Wife briefly, the slender profile of her body outlined by the moon in the darkness, and sent out one more prayer to Min to flood her birth-cave with the fertile silt in which people grow. Then he lay back, adjusting his headrest as quietly as he could, and listened to the sound of Horemheb's celebration. It seemed like months, not hours, since they had left the party, gracing only its beginning with the royal presence.

He continued to lie awake until the sounds of carousal had died away, to be replaced soon after by the muted shuffling and suppressed coughing of the palace servants as they rose, lit fires for cooking, fetched water, milk, beans and flour for the first meal, and brought the palace to life. Soon, the body servants would come to awaken them and bathe them, and the chief steward would arrive with the private secretary, both to receive and give the domestic and public orders for the day. To be so shackled to duty without the reward of power was beginning to kill the king's *Ka*. Behind all the other noises came the call of egrets by the river. Tutankhamun's strained eyes continued to stare into the gathering day. Lightheaded, hungover from lack of sleep, his mouth dry, he sat inside himself and tried to listen to what his heart would tell him.

'Be a prisoner no longer. The only way out is to kill the jailer.'

He had heard the words before, many times. He wondered how long it would be before he stopped listening and started to act. Well, he had made a start, of sorts, and he knew that he could not spend the rest of his life waking into agony. Despite himself, he found himself thinking of the old king, Akhenaten.

How valuable his advice would be be now! Tutankhamun tried to remember that remote, fatherly, fragile creature, but the edges of his memory were blurred and he could conjure up a body but no face. An impression of gentleness and comfort remained.

The king swung his feet off the bed and stood in one lithe movement, making his head spin. He heard body servants approaching and saw them hovering in the curtained doorway, not daring to enter as they noticed the queen still sleeping. He picked up a linen wrap from the back of a black wood-and-gilt folding chair and tied it round him, approaching the door.

'Mesesia,' he said to one of them, beckoning. The man came forward a few paces, his shaven head bowed.

'Go and find Ahmose,' said the king. 'Bring him to the Red Room and tell him to wait for me there.'

Some time later, after the conclusion of the interview, Ahmose made his way out of the palace by a side entrance. He had not talked of much with the king. It had seemed to him that all Tutankhamun wanted to do was bolster his confidence by once more going over and refining his plan to assassinate Horemheb. Ahmose, a courtier for seventeen years, and a man whose solid, avuncular presence had served him well in the matter of eliciting secrets, congratulated himself that the king still seemed to regard him as a member of his inner circle. It was a nuisance that the young man was too clever to allow the members of it to know each other. For a time Ahmose had wondered if the king mistrusted him; then he had wondered if the whole conspiracy against the general was not a simple fantasy. Now he was sure that some loose form of revolution was being prepared. Patience would bring him the details, and perhaps even the names of the conspirators.

Leaving the outer courtyard of the palace, he turned round once to look up at the columned gallery which ran along the first storey. He could see no one there. He turned again and set off at a brisker pace.

16

From behind the column against which he was leaning, the king watched the fat courtier turn, and scurry through the gate, hesitating for only a fraction of a second before taking the street which led in the direction of Horemheb's overblown house. Tutankhamun clenched his fist. This battle would not be soon won. But he was learning, all the time.

# THREE

The king accepted in his heart that unless they were helped, the gods would remain impartial. As the present custodian of the perpetual incarnation of Ra-on-Earth, he did not hesitate. And to his joy, but hardly to his surprise, one action by him triggered others by those gods whose alliance he had solicited for so long.

He meant Ahmose's death as a warning, however oblique, to the general. He had the man abducted and drowned downriver, reluctant to accord him anything other than a merciful, noble death. Then he had the body brought back to the city and laid on the shore near Horemheb's jetty. It was a custom which he followed, rather than initiated, and he was sure that the general would read the shorthand correctly. His worry stemmed from not knowing how many other Ahmoses there were in his camp.

Anxiety turned to triumph later, though he still had several months to wait, during which neither side – Tutankhamun had begun to think of the series of moves and counter-moves as a cold war – did more than wait, watchfully maintaining their positions on the board. Then the gods suddenly struck two blows in his favour.

The year had turned round and the Black Land had entered the season of *shemu* again. After the enervating activity of the harvest, which in this good year had filled the granaries and taken even the workers from the valley, where the great tombs of the departed lay on the west bank of the River across from the Southern Capital, to help gather the generous crop of emmer, barley and flax, the country lay in grateful exhaustion. The king's heart could not rest, though, because it dwelt with an unwelcome tirelessness on the fact of his wife's empty birth-cave, and on the imminent gift from Nut and Geb of a child to Horemheb and Nezemmut. It took two seasons and one passage of the moon for a child to grow in the birth-cave, and the time was almost up.

But Nezemmut's child was born early and dead. To the king's secret satisfaction, it had been a boy. That would be vinegar on the general's lips. The little corpse, with its huge head, curled like a baby crocodile in the egg, was swiftly dried and embalmed, and set aside in a cedar box for the time to come when it would join its unlucky parents in their tomb. They would know the same pain the king had.

The next month Ankhsi's bleeding stopped. She showed Tutankhamun the linen towel. It was as clean as when her maid had bound it to her loins. The king hardly dared breathe.

The news quickly spread from a household which had been divided between hope and despair for years now. Happy body servants told their wives, husbands and lovers – there was no interdict of secrecy from the king. Sorrow at the queen's dead womb gave way to speculation about the royal child's sex. The betting odds down in the harbour quarter settled cautiously in favour of a son, and the former scribe Huy put a golden piece down in the hope of a male child. The sunlight at long last seemed to move across the palace compound and settle on the king's house instead of Horemheb's. The general and his household made their congratulations, and the king formally commiserated with their misfortune. Both publicly accepted the will of the gods, and secretly made contingency plans.

At first Tutankhamun was fearful that he had tempted the gods' anger by premature celebration, but a second month passed and the linen wad was as free of dark blood as ever. The queen's guard was doubled, and Horemheb's special Medjays were banished from the precincts of the palace. The general wore a fixed expression, and was seen less in public. Ay, on the other hand, became a more frequent visitor to the king.

By the third month, the pharaoh decided he had been away from the hunt long enough.

'You must be careful.' Ankhsenpaamun had never liked hunting. It was dangerous and bloody. The king was half a stranger for a hour after his return. Sometimes he was away for weeks.

'Don't worry.'

'How long will you be gone?'

'Three days at the most.'

'And where will you go?'

'Where the quarry lies.'

'What will you hunt?'

'It depends what we see. I want to fetch something special for you.'

'Do not hunt lions,' said the queen. She was fearful of the new, light chariot. It was faster, she knew, than many of the animals the king loved to chase, but she also knew that it overturned easily. If the king fell near a furious wounded animal like a lion, or, worse, a wild bull, he would die. Alone, she knew she would not be able to stand up to their enemies. Like her sisters, she would be condemned to a luxurious prison and an empty life. Or, worse, there was the threat of marriage to Ay.

'Do not go unattended,' she added. 'Take many bowmen with you.'

'Of course,' the king reassured her. Privately, he had it in mind to hunt lion. His ancestor Nebmare Amenophis had bagged one hundred as a young man. It was his ambition to pass that record.

He went to inspect his animals. His lean hunting dogs bounded to the gates of their pen to see him, jostling each other to put their great sand-running paws against the wooden crossbar,

20

thrusting eager heads forward, red tongues flickering in open mouths, brown eyes keen, long tails wagging. He stroked their soft ears and cradled their pointed snouts.

The cats, trained to retrieve fish and small game-birds, were more sedate, but they left off washing, and their ears became alert as they paced the limits of their pens, occasionally scrapping with one another. Nearby, his two cheetahs, captured young and trained for the chase by Nubian huntsmen, stretched and eyed him half watchfully, half expectantly. He paused to reprimand their beast-slave for not yet refreshing their water that day, then made his way to the far end of the vast cedar enclosure, to where his riding and chariot horses were corralled.

These costly animals, the third generation to be bred in the south, were the king's pride and joy. He adored their strength and their loyalty, and they were guarded with almost as great care as himself. He gave them slivers of honey cake, and real apples expensively imported from the lands to the north.

'What game is there?' he asked his chief huntsman.

'Nearby, ibex, gazelle. Plenty of ibex, not half a day's ride.'

'I am interested in lions, Nehesy.'

The man considered. 'Not near. It is too dry now. Perhaps south of the First Cataract, or out by the Dakhla Oasis.'

The king shook his head, disappointed. Both places were too far away. He thought of the half-promise he had given Ankhsi not to be absent longer. He wanted to bring her back trophies worthy of a king, knowing that the spirits of the animals would enter him, their vanquisher, and build his strength; but he was anxious too that she should not be alone too long. Since the Ahmose episode the king had not known whom to trust, and he had given orders to his personal guard that only blood relatives should be allowed to see her; but he knew he could not deny access to Horemheb or Ay.

'Are you sure there are none nearer?'

'If you took the horses by river you could be at the First Cataract in two days.'

'It is still too long.'

'How long does the king intend to hunt?'

'I cannot spare more than three days.'

'It is a pity we have no lions corralled.'

'That is not hunting,' said the king contemptuously. Very seldom now did any of the nobles hunt in the old way, spearing animals already trapped in a corral from the top of the palisade. The horse and the light electrum chariot had brought speed and mobility and danger to the sport.

'Will you hunt on the River?' suggested Nehesy, seeing the tightness on the king's face, which however quickly recovered its customary, dangerously bland expression. 'I could call the wildfowlers. Or perhaps we could go after river-horse or crocodile?'

'No. I want to use the chariot. We will go after ibex. Where are the good herds?'

'They are in the Eastern Desert.'

'Good. We will save time by not having to cross the River.'

'When shall we go?'

'As soon as the heat of the day is past. I will take my usual team and the new chariot.'

'And what dogs?'

'Give me Pepi, Ypu and Ruttet. Sherybin will be my charioteer.'

The king spent the rest of the morning pleasurably choosing hunting spears, and discussing with Nehesy and Sherybin the best bows to take. The new chariot was drawn out into the yard and propped up on its shaft, gleaming red-gold in the sun while they tested the leather footstraps and handholds for firmness. They discussed the pros and cons of the machine's heavier floor, which created greater stability at the expense of speed.

'But we will not need so much speed for ibex,' said Sherybin.

'I know,' replied the king, sullenly.

'There is a bull in the herd with the finest horns I have ever

22

seen,' Nehesy put in quickly. 'I can see them now on the prow of your falcon-ship.'

'Good,' the king responded, brightening.

'Who else will you take with you?' asked Nehesy.

'You will come, and the three best trackers, and with you, two more chariots. Put my men in them.'

'Is that enough protection?'

'It should be. I am not going after dangerous beasts.'

'No,' Nehesy hesitated. 'I meant . . .' He trailed off, not knowing how to finish.

Tutankhamun looked at him. 'What do you mean?'

He spread his hands. 'With a child on the way, your safety is important.'

The pharaoh considered. 'Three chariots then. And my strongest men in them. We will not be away long.'

He left them, but he could not shake off irritation. The security arrangements cast a shadow over his enjoyment. Hunting was the one time he tried to forget he was a king, entrapped in the net of intrigue and duty which seemed to press closer on him with every day that passed. Irrational as he knew it was, he longed for once to go out into the desert alone, to shake off other people, and to pit himself against the forces of the wild.

He took the midday food with the queen alone, eating frugally and simply: some *ful* with salted curds and plain bread. Then they went to the bedchamber to sleep. She stroked him as they lay naked in the brown twilight behind the closed shutters of the room, and he responded to her, slipping an arm around her and pulling her to him, squeezing her narrow buttocks with his hand. Then he lay back and allowed her to mount him, as she liked to, and she rode him with sleepy gentleness for half an hour before he surged into her and she bent and clung to his neck, moaning. In the peace which followed, he forgot his other anxieties and yearnings – or at least, the fulfilment of lovemaking forced them to retreat to the far corners of his heart.

23

The body servants came for him at the tenth hour of day, as the sun was inclining steeply towards the cliffs of the valley on the opposite bank of the river, and they changed colour from ochre to red to black. Ankhsi rose with him and bathed him herself. He could feel her unhappiness like a wall between them, and it diminished his own anticipation of the hunt. After all, a part of his heart whispered to him, they were only going after ibex. But having made his decision he would not change his mind; and he was proud of his reputation as a keen and accomplished hunter. Still he could not shake off the power of her reproach, and he disliked the way she clung to him when they parted.

'Have the gods spoken to you?' He asked her softly, one eye on the body servants who stood near.

'No.'

'No warning?'

'If there had been, I would tell you. You would not go.'

'To whom have you prayed?'

'To Hathor and Onuris.' To the Suckler of the King and the Huntsman. The same gods as the king had chosen. It was a good omen. Tutankhamun smiled, kissed his wife again, on the nose, eyes, ears and lips, and touched the lower gates of her body lightly with his hand.

'May they keep you,' he said.

'May they keep you indeed,' she returned, looking at him sadly.

As soon as he was away from her he felt relieved, the burden of her reproach lifted by her absence. The warm wind on his face as he rode into the desert rushed through his being and cleansed his heart. Under Sherybin's control, the excited horses skimmed across the firm sand, and the king was free to scan the twilight landscape as it swept by like the sea.

They pitched camp at dusk, gathering round the fire to eat as the first watch was set. The tents were frail and vulnerable in the vastness of the desert, their linen sides flapping in a

24

rough wind that eddied round, changing direction abruptly, whipping sand into their faces, and making shadows leap. In the silence that followed it, Tutankhamun listened hopefully for lions, but nothing came out of the darkness except the lonely bark of a distant jackal. Nehesy and Sherybin were men of his age, Sherybin younger, and he rejoiced in their company. If only the quarry were more exciting! He insisted that they retire before he did, and remained by the fire as it died, as alone as he ever would be, he thought, with only a guard and a body servant for company. He opened his heart to the great emptiness around him and let it take possession of him.

The following day the trackers, who had left before dawn to lope silently into the gloom to the east, returned to report a small herd of ibex – fifteen to twenty – in a cluster of low hills – no more than large rocks – half an hour's ride ahead. The four chariots of the hunting group were harnessed to their teams and set off – the king and Sherybin in the lead, with Nehesy and his charioteer off to the right, and the two others riding to the left and rear. They were well spread out, to confuse the focus of their prey. Tutankhamun weighed a medium spear in his hand and suppressed the thought of lions.

Soon enough the rocks came into view, looming grey against the yellow of the desert. Years ago a small gold mine had been worked here, but now all that remained of it was a cave-like opening among the rocks, and the broken remains of water jars. They were not far off the main route from the Southern Capital to the port on the Eastern Sea from where the swift coasters departed for Punt, but the desolation of the desert covered them like a pall. The chariots fanned out and, the horses slowed to a trot, rode round the rocks at a distance. From the jagged grey shapes, softer ones began to detach themselves as the large, brown-grey animals raised their heads with the great swept-back horns to regard this intrusion with curiosity and caution.

The king exchanged his spear for a bow and arrow. Nodding

to Sherybin, he steadied himself in the footstrap on the floor of the chariot and drew on his archer's glove.

The hunt lasted all morning, but it was not a success. Three animals lay drawn up on the sand, but they were elderly, only having fallen prey to the archers because they had lost their nimbleness. There was no honour in their deaths, and the king had called off the pursuit in disgust. This was not the way to celebrate the arrival of his child. He returned moodily to camp. His humour was not improved by news from Sherybin that his chariot had a damaged axle, and that a new one would have to be brought from the capital; but he gave his charioteer permission to absent himself from the hunt for the second day in order to fetch the spare part. On that day he hunted with Nehesy, but the only living thing they saw were golden desert rats which popped up from their holes to gawp at them.

On the last day the king was awakened early by an excited Sherybin.

'The trackers have brought news,' said the charioteer, scarcely able to contain his enthusiasm.

'Of what?' The king squinted past him at the sky outside the tent. Could the trackers be back already?

'Wild cattle,' Sherybin told him in a triumphant whisper.

Tutankhamun's heart leapt. If the news were true, then the omen had been good after all. Wild cattle! That would be a prize worthy of the great Tuthmosis himself. Only the pharaohs were allowed to hunt them, and if he could bring down a bull . . .!

His ambitions raced ahead of him.

'Waken the others. We must set off immediately.'

Sherybin quietened him. For a moment they were two excited men, equals, eagerly discussing the merits of an important hunt. 'No. Not the others. You know how nervous wild cattle are. If we go in a big group we might panic them and then they'd be gone before we could get one decent shot at them.'

'But if we go alone we'll have fewer chances of getting anything.'

'More than a group would ever have. I know your shooting. You are the best in the Black Land.'

Tutankhamun had trained himself to bite the metal of flattery to see if it was good. But coming from so experienced a hunter and charioteer as Sherybin, this was to be taken as a compliment without question.

'We will leave word with one of the guards to say what direction we have taken,' continued Sherybin, allaying the king's other unspoken fear without being asked. 'Come, if we delay we will miss our chance. They must be crossing the desert from oasis to oasis and they will not be caught in the open once the sun is high.'

Convinced, the king rose, washing and dressing at speed, strapping on his leather armguard himself, and brushing aside the attentions of his body servant. He stepped out of the tent into the keen blue night and the cool silence of the desert. No one stirred, though not far from the encampment he was surprised to see his chariot ready harnessed, one of the trackers standing by the horses. Sherybin spoke swiftly and urgently to a guard as he came forward into the glow from the fire, and then helped the king on to the footplate of the chariot, where the right weapons were ranged ready. The long-limbed tracker ran ahead, soon barely visible in the gloom, taking a southerly direction. They followed at an unhurried trot, making as little noise as possible. The king took a last look at the sleeping camp, but the thought of wild cattle dispelled any lingering doubts in his heart. He turned his face to the wind and imagined brown-and-white hides, proud jet-black eyes, and long, crooked horns.

The tracker was out of sight now. Clicking to the horses, Sherybin encouraged them to a canter. Tutankhamun grasped the leather handstrap more firmly, and cast his eye over the weapons. A heavy throwing spear, a sturdier bow than he had used on the first day, and a bronze short-sword in a leather scabbard. The horses moved faster now across the featureless desert, but somehow the tracker must have kept ahead, for the

27

king did not see him. Then, coldly, the thought came to him that Sherybin could not see him either, and if that were so, how did he know what direction to take? He looked covertly at his charioteer, who did not return the glance, even if he were aware of it, but kept his eyes ahead.

'How much further?' asked the king. A thin line of pale blue outlined the low hills near the coast away to the east and he knew that very soon there would be light enough to see for miles. He gauged the speed with which he could draw the sword. With the dawn came a gathering wind from the north.

'Soon,' came the reply. The voice was still warm and enthusiastic, even carrying with it some of the tension of the hunt. But the king's belly told him what a fool he had been.

'Where is the tracker?'

'Ahead.'

'No tracker could run that fast.'

Sherybin drew the chariot up. 'Listen.'

At first, after the noise of the horses' hooves and the clattering of the chariot, the silence seemed impenetrable. But then, out of it, distant at first, came the noise of other hooves. The king peered ahead into the gloaming from where the sounds came, and as he watched dark shapes began to detach themselves from it, crossing the path ahead. The king's breath came faster. He felt himself becoming transfixed and forced himself to turn, to see what Sherybin was doing. He was just in time. His charioteer's hand was on the haft of the sword.

Without thinking, the king brought his own right fist smashing down. The three heavy gold rings crushed the bones of the thin brown hand beneath them, and the charioteer drew away with a hiss of pain. Tutankhamun brought the sword out of the scabbard in one sharp movement and held it at Sherybin's throat.

'What have you done?' he said.

The man smiled wanly, but there was fear in his eyes.

'You should not have driven so fast,' continued the pharaoh.

'I might never have suspected anything.' He was surprised at his own calm, as from the corner of his eye he saw the shapes approach, still too far away to identify individually, but in the gathering light were certainly not cattle. Horsemen. Could they see what had happened on the chariot? They were approaching without haste.

He tried to calculate how far from the camp they had come. Sound travelled a long way in the desert, especially in the thin air of morning. Whatever happened now, would happen fast.

He seized the reins from his charioteer's numb left hand, and raised the sword, at the same time pushing his foot firmly into the footstrap for balance.

'May Set swallow you, Sherybin,' he said, pronouncing the curse precisely, without emotion. Fear and – possibly – shame had turned the charioteer into a statue. Thoughts flew through the king's heart. He wanted to say more, to find out why. Above all he was appalled at the betrayal and at the speed with which it had taken place. He had little doubt of its originator. But there was no time. The horsemen were approaching, and they were doing so faster. He brought the sword down hard. The blade cut the base of Sherybin's muscular young neck and cleaved through the collar bone down to the sternum. The charioteer was still gaping and gagging, his hands jerking up to the wound, when the king, leaving the sword where it had jammed, thrust him off the chariot with his elbow.

The horses were uneasy. Trying to keep his own voice steady to calm them, Tutankhamun turned them. The riders were not a hundred paces away now, and he could hear them calling to each other. They had seen Sherybin fall. The chariot's turn, accomplished in a second during the hunt, now took an age, but at last it was done. The king took a firm grip of the reins and held them taut so that the horses' heads reared. With his free hand he took up the spear. Then, gathering air in his lungs, he lashed the horses forward and sped back towards the camp, roaring his battle cry as he did so. Behind him, he could hear the sound of hooves as his pursuers whipped their mounts forward. How many of them were there? Ten? Twenty?

He flew, but as he continued to cry out he knew that the north wind was blowing the sound of his ever-weakening voice back to the men behind him. Nehesy would never hear him at the camp. But by now they would be up, and perhaps even saddled and riding after him. It had been clever of Sherybin to give directions to a guard, but perhaps over-confident. The thought gave the king new heart.

Then one of his horses stumbled, and though it recovered almost immediately, the chariot had slewed round and the king knew that he had lost fatal seconds by the time he was back on course. His heart became hollow as from the corner of his eye he could see a rider gaining on his flank. He yelled encouragement at the horses and once more the light chariot flew forwards. Tutankhamun gulped air, part of him caught in a wild thrill that had little to do with the horror of his situation. He could not believe that he would die, that anyone would dare to perpetrate, plan or even imagine bringing about the death of a pharaoh. Such an act was to kill god. But through the mists of his flying thoughts came a clear one of his immediate predecessor Smenkhkare, who had died suddenly at the age of twenty, in the midst of life. How?

He brought his senses back to his own race with death. A dark figure was riding close to his horses now, stooping to grasp their head harness. He pulled his horses back to slow them of his own accord, throwing the rider off balance, and, drawing his right arm back, thrust the spear forward blindly. He felt its point catch weight and dig in, and then the end of the shaft he held was pulled out of his hand as the figure impaled on its end soundlessly dropped from his mount, which veered away into the open desert.

Tutankhamun looked ahead, but the rush of wind in his face forced him to keep his eyes screwed tight, and he could see little. There was no sign of the camp or of Nehesy riding to help him. A grain of sand caught in his left eye and made him

30

close it, involuntarily slowing again. His heart told him it was over. He could sense them on either side of the chariot now, and his own horses giving him up as they lost the will to run. He had no weapon left which he could use at close quarters.

The death of their fellow had been to their gain, because killing him had cost Tutankhamun the final seconds of advantage he had. They had both his horses by the head now, leaning back on their mounts to slow the chariot, digging in with leg muscles like rope to the brown flanks.

One more yell produced a last flagging effort from his horses, but they were beyond obedience now, frightened and confused. He felt that reality was receding from him. As if in a dream he watched his team dragged to a halt, lowering their heads as they were released, submissive, done. From behind him at last a voice issued one harsh and laconic order:

'Quickly.'

Tutankhamun's heart acknowledged that he had heard the voice of death, but still the events around him seemed to have nothing to do with him. He stood in the chariot like the captain of a sinking riverboat, watching as the horses were hastily unhitched. The tilting of the shaft downwards as they were withdrawn and the men holding it lowered it to the sand made him stagger. Then, in the precise second before he was seized and dragged from his place, reality flooded him, and in a moment of anguish he saw Anhksi again, whom he would never see again, whose warm breath he would never again feel on his chest as she slept. He thought of the child he would never know, and the kingdom he would never rule. How had he been so cruelly out-manoeuvred? He had been so careful!

A last thought crossed his heart: if he could not live as a king, he would at least die like one. He plucked an arrow from the quiver just as they laid hands on him, and flung it at the rider whose voice, it appeared to him, had issued the order; a thin, angular man with a scant beard. Its flight was true, and for a glorious, hopeful moment it looked as if it might strike him in the eye. But it fell short. Tutankhamun had time to see it dash against his right cheek, drawing blood, before they pulled him down.

Now he no longer seemed to be part of his body. He watched from somewhere in the air above as they forced it to its knees, pinioning its arms. Two men did this, destroying their hearts and souls for all eternity as they committed the crime. He could not see their faces; indeed did not want to. Two other men were overturning the chariot with feverish haste. Two more were slinging the body of the man he had killed over his horse, which they had recaptured. He could see how the wind, which had borne his voice away from his friends, was blowing sand over the mess of their tracks. By the time Nehesy arrived, there would be no sign of what had happened. Except for Sherybin. What would they do with him?

But as he watched, more horsemen, working in the same hasty silence, dragged the charioteer's body up. His wound was split over one wheel of the machine, as if he had fallen on it in the accident. The sword was cleaned carefully and stowed in its place on the chariot. Still the wind continued its work as accomplice, erasing the traces as they appeared.

Then the voice spoke again. There was tightness in it, but he could not tell, nor did he care, whether the tone stemmed from anger at the wound or increased urgency.

'Quickly.'

It occurred to him at last that they had not stopped his mouth. He was still bent forward, held, and he could not fill his lungs. But he opened his mouth and started to bellow his war cry. Suddenly it was a desperate cry for life. Ankhsi appeared before him so vividly that he could smell her, taste her soft body, bury his head in her breast. The yearning was unbearable.

Then the blow fell, and, before the darkness came, all he could feel were the sand in his nostrils and a trickle of blood on his face.

# FOUR

'It was an accident?'

'A hunting accident. Yes. Most tragic.'

Huy looked out of the broad window of the room towards a columned gallery, beyond which the sun hung in a hard blue sky. Below, the river ran between its dun banks, crowded on this side with the jumble of mean houses that formed the district where Huy lived.

Much had happened in the two days which had passed since the hunting party had secretly brought the king's body back, although no public announcements had been made by the newsbreakers. That Huy was being given privileged information had been impressed upon him at the beginning of this interview. But the city was already full of rumours, and there was an indefinable tension in the air, which Huy had even picked up in the harbour quarter, where people's concern for the pharaoh was slight.

Now, he tried to absorb the shock of the king's death. He looked at Ay, standing by the window. In age, Ay had grown a paunch, but his bird-like, intellectual head had barely changed. There were wrinkles, and the hairline had receded; but the hair was dyed dark, and Huy would have had no difficulty in recognising the man he had known, distantly, at the City of the Horizon.

'When will the news be broken?' Huy asked.

'It must be soon. You are aware how people are beginning to fear something. Neither the king or queen have been seen in public, and that will strike everyone as strange, especially

33

after the announcement of the queen's pregnancy.' Ay spoke with formal stiffness, which Huy supposed had become a habit after years in politics.

'Why has it been delayed?'

Ay shook his head. 'Horemheb has decreed it. Of course, he tells me it is for reasons of security. But if the king's death was simply a question of a tragic accident, what reason could there be for secrecy?'

Huy reflected that the wheel had come full circle, and tried to deduce what Ay was deliberately omitting from his account. In the old days, at the City of the Horizon, Huy had been a scribe in the legal section of Akhenaten's court, and now and then had to do with colleagues attached to Ay's office. After the fall of Akhenaten, and the ruin of his city, Huy imagined that Ay must either have died, or escaped into one of the friendly neighbouring countries – Mitanni or Babylon, perhaps – to live out his life in self-imposed exile. But even before the court had returned to the Southern Capital, Huy had seen Ay with Horemheb escorting the young Tutankhamun to the ritual of Opening the Mouth of his predecessor, Smenkhkare. Ay was clearly a survivor.

Huy had returned to the Southern Capital himself soon after, and, forbidden to continue to practise as a scribe because of his association with the disgraced Akhenaten, he had turned, partly by chance, to solving the kind of problems people had which they did not wish the Medjays involved with. His association with the great men of the city a few years earlier seemed to have borne fruit at last. Now he had been summoned to Ay's presence in secret, on the recommendation of his former employer Ipuky, another man who had managed to escape unscathed after the fall of Akhenaten.

And now Ay was asking him to solve a problem. At least it looked as if the conversation was going that way. Quickly Huy ran through what Ay had told him.

Two days earlier, Nehesy and the hunting party which had accompanied the king into the desert had returned with his chariot and horses, and the bodies of the king and his charioteer. Knowing what the public outcry would be if he rode openly into the city, and scared about his own fate as the professional in charge of the expedition, Nehesy had made sure to return at nightfall. He had then gone straight to Horemheb with the news of what had happened.

'What happened then?' Huy asked the old man. They were both seated by a low table on which wine and dates had been placed, more as a gesture than genuine hospitality. What they had to talk about was too serious to be discussed over food and drink.

Ay shrugged briefly. 'All the information I can give you is what I was told by Horemheb, so bear that in mind. Of course he had to share the news with me immediately. I had just retired to read when his messenger came to fetch me.'

'Where were the bodies?'

'We had them both taken back to the palace. The charioteer was laid out in his quarters and the king was placed in the audience chamber. The first thing to do was summon doctors, and then tell the queen.'

Huy shifted in his chair. 'Of course.' It occurred to him that the queen's isolation was not only to the advantage of Horemheb, but Ay's as well. Ay had no son; but Huy had a shrewd idea that the limit of his ambition would not be reached by seeing his daughter Nezemmut as queen; and if Horemheb had recently lost a son, Ay had lost a grandson. Nezemmut could have more children. Ay could take a younger wife if he chose and try to father sons himself. Neither he nor Horemheb would want to run the risk of seeing Ankhsenpaamun give successful birth at last to a male child.

'How is the queen?' he asked.

'Distraught,' replied Ay.

'What will happen to her?'

Ay looked surprised. 'What should happen to her? She will remain in the palace. She carries the future pharaoh, perhaps.

The gods may even decree that if a girl-child is born she will reign as king. It has happened before.'

'And in the meantime?'

Ay avoided looking at him. 'That has yet to be discussed. We must ask the gods for guidance. I imagine . . . a new regency . . . as a temporary measure, for the stability of the country. Unlike Smenkhkare, the king died leaving no close relative to whom the crown may be given, except for the still-to-be-born in the queen's birth-cave.'

'How did the accident happen?' asked Huy.

'That I do not know. But I have seen the wounds. They are ghastly. The charioteer was almost cut in two by one of the wheels.'

'And the king?'

'He must have been thrown clear when the chariot capsized, and struck his head on a rock.' Ay paused.

'Those are the doctors' conclusions?'

'Yes. They are self-evident. And there is no reason, really, to suspect anything other than an accident – though what the pharaoh was doing out hunting alone with his charioteer is still a mystery. Still, there are no grounds for believing it was the fault of the rest of the hunting party, and so they have been spared death.' Ay poured wine and drank it in hurried sips. Huy saw that his lower lip was moist and slack.

The former scribe paused in thought before speaking again. 'What a tragedy this is,' he said formally. 'For the king's family, and for the country.'

'Indeed,' replied Ay. 'And the queen is left alone.'

Huy waited in the silence, wondering what was coming next; but the old man appeared to expect him to speak.

'What do you want me to do?' he asked.

Ay leant forward. 'Despite all the evidence, I do not believe this was an accident. Too much is at stake. It reeks of coincidence. I want you to find out what really happened. I can fund you, and I can give you names; but I cannot help you more than that. Do you understand?'

'Yes.'

'Will you do it?'

'It will be difficult.'

Ay smiled. 'I have not heard that difficulty deters you.'

'Let me make plans, and then I will report to you.'

Ay waved a querulous hand. 'I do not wish to know your plans, and your contact with me must remain secret. I will send my messenger to you when I consider it safe to do so. Everything you do you must do as discreetly as possible. I chose you because I trust Ipuky, and because despite your obvious worth you are little known in this city.'

'What is your objective?'

Ay looked at him. 'If you accept this job, I become your employer. My objective should not concern you. But you are an intelligent man and you will draw your own conclusions. Be sure that I will reward loyalty, Huy; just as certainly as I will punish betrayal.'

'I will need access to the palace compound.'

'I can arrange that. But you may not wear my livery. Nothing must connect you with me. I will have you attached to the palace as a house priest's assistant. They will be preparing the king's *Book of the Dead* for him to take to the tomb.'

'What must I do? I cannot work as a scribe.'

'I know that, Huy. You will probably have to do nothing. There are many servants in the palace in that position. The important thing is that the badge of office will get you past the guards.'

'I will have to talk to the huntsman. I will have to see the chariot, and visit the place where the accident happened.'

'All that is clear to me. How you do it, however, is your problem.'

Public events hurried the next days past, making it impossible for Huy to do more than lay outline plans and digest what he had been told. It was clear that he was about to wade in deeper water than he had ever entered before; and he trusted

37

his paymaster no more than anyone else who might have been involved in the king's death. If it had not been an accident . . . There was nothing yet to suggest that it had been anything else, and possibly only Ay's devious mind would see intrigue where there was none.

When the death was announced, messengers on horseback – faster than river boats – were dispatched to the north and south to carry the news as far as the Delta and Meroe. The city prepared itself for the initial period of mourning which would last for the seventy days the embalmers took to prepare the body for the grave. In the meantime, many additional teams of workmen were exempted from mourning inactivity and sent to the valley to speed up the work on the king's tomb, which would be by no means ready to receive him properly, as work on it had only been in progress since his accession nine years earlier, but which would have to fulfil its function as best it could. There were some who thought the haste with which this work was set in motion indecent, but as the orders were issued from the palace itself no one could criticise them openly.

Huy found the hurry interesting: Tutankhamun was, it appeared, going to get little of the dignity which was normally associated with the burial of a monarch. He watched as hastily from one quarter and another of the country the funeral offerings and furniture were gathered together under the quartermaster of the royal tombs. They were displayed on public view for a month before being consigned to the burial chamber. Huy went to look at them, and it grieved him to see what poor stuff it was. Some of the trappings had been lifted brazenly from Smenkhkare's burial, and though the workmanship and the carving and the volume of precious metal and stone befitted a king, Huy, who, as a child, remembered watching the great entombment of Nebmare Amenophis, was sorry to see how dismissively the young pharaoh was being treated. He was certain that if it had been within her power, Tutankhamun's widow would have taken steps to prevent such cut-price treatment.

Shabbily dressed, Huy crossed the River by one of the black ferry boats and visited the tomb builders. Most, caked with sweat and dust, were too busy to talk, but he recognised one overseer whose acquaintance he had made years earlier, and who remembered him.

'Good day,' said the man, looking at him. 'It's been years. You don't look as if they have been kind.'

'I manage.'

'That's just about what I'd call it, to look at you. Have a drink.'

They retired to the shelter of an awning made of an old tarpaulin stretched over driftwood stakes, and the overseer broke the clay seals off two jars of black beer he had resting in a water jug to keep them cool. They drank in silence, looking down over the scorching valley to the sluggish river below. The season was progressing. Perhaps some of the haste was due to the need to get the king buried before the flood came. Already, barely distinguishable, there were traces of the telltale red sand in the water.

'How is the work?'

'It's a rush job,' said the overseer. 'But the main tunnelling was done already, so it's been a question of plastering and painting. And a lot of that was at least sketched out, so it won't look too terrible by the time we're finished.'

'May I see?'

The overseer laughed. 'Quite a student of these things, aren't you? You can see the antechamber. Beyond that, the layout's secret.'

Acknowledging this, Huy finished his beer and entered the tomb. Inside, it was cool, though the men working by the light of oil lamps glistened with sweat. He came across one mural which was fresh, the outline only just worked out, with the painter just starting on the colouring. It showed a large group. Ay, depicted, as he always liked to be, as a vigorous young man, and dressed in regalia which came very close to those of a king, was performing the ritual of the Opening of the Mouth upon Tutankhamun.

As a mark of respect, the picture was blameless. But Huy found it disturbing that Ay – on whose orders it must have been made – had accorded himself the honour which should fall to the pharaoh's successor.

'Do you know when this painting was planned?' Huy asked the man working on it, a plump fellow with pendulous breasts and a careful eye.

The artist looked at Huy briefly. 'Since the king died,' he replied in an undertone, before turning all of his attention back to his work.

Huy made his way home thoughtfully, grateful for the cool and solitude of his little house. He changed out of his workman's disguise and bathed, wondering what the significance of the painting might be. There was no representation of Horemheb at all in the tomb; but that could be explained by the fact that the general had only just married, peripherally, into the royal household, and, also perhaps that, secure in the knowledge of his power, he had preferred to remain aloof. But Ay appeared to be indulging in vulgar, pre-emptive and over-anxious claim-staking. Perhaps by it he hoped to win the favour of the pharaoh's *Ka*. It was certainly true that the richest among the funeral gifts had been donated by him. If Horemheb and Ay were engaged in a race for the throne, then Ay had the stronger claim; but his power was less. Caught in the middle would be the queen.

The more Huy thought about her, the more her situation worried him. If she were not adequately protected, she could be plucked out of history leaving no trace behind. Her aunt was unlikely to intercede for her, and although Ay was her grandfather, the family tie was too remote to weigh in the balance against his ambition. He was her potential ally, but that was cold comfort, for if Ay gained the throne he would not be likely to show mercy to the parent of the rightful heir.

\*      \*      \*

The first day at the palace Huy kept his head down, watching. He had arrived to find that he was attached to no particular house priest, but the bustle and activity was such that no one noticed or cared. One guard was suspicious when he saw Huy hanging about in an inner courtyard for longer than seemed necessary, but he was immediately reassured by the badge of office the former scribe showed him. The guard was a young man, and Huy wondered drily whether it was not just the badge, but the fact that it was worn by a thickset thirty-five-year-old with the muscles of a riverman. It was not the first time that he'd had to thank his unprepossessing but tough appearance, that went with neither his profession nor his nature.

The palace itself was an intricate warren of rooms and interconnected buildings, and the day was well advanced before Huy was able to find his way to the quarters occupied by the huntsmen. In his search for them he had noticed a heavy guard on the audience chamber, where the king's body still lay, packed in fresh dampened linen which was replaced hourly, awaiting the moment – soon – when it would be taken through the palace to the open-ended, narrow building that housed the royal embalmers. Here the process of preparing the king for eternity would begin, leaving a wrapped and dried husk asleep in three layers of gilded cedarwood seventy days later.

The huntsmen's quarters were near the stables by the river on the western side of the palace, some distance from the royal buildings. There was a great cedar shed to house the animals, and beyond it a corral for the horses. Six of them moved about restlessly as he passed it. Seven low dwellings formed a rough protective crescent behind the corral, the central one of which was larger than the others. Accompanied by two of the palace guards, four men were loading a shrouded body on to a long, narrow ox-cart which stood next to the house at the northern end of the crescent. As Huy watched, they lowered it gently on to the floor of the cart and covered it with palm boughs. Then one of the men clicked at the oxen, who began plodding towards a road which led away to the north-east, the direction from which Huy had come.

He was hot and footsore, for he had lost his way twice in getting here. There were two other men in sight, both stableboys by the look of them. One approached him, looking curious. Huy displayed his badge of office.

'I'm looking for Nehesy,' he said.

'Who wants him?'

'I do. I've come from the palace. It's about the king's dogs,' said Huy.

'Yes?'

'They will be needed for the procession.'

'That won't be for two months.'

'You don't understand,' replied Huy loftily. 'Everything has to be taken into account well in advance, not scrabbled together at the last moment. And who do you think you're talking to anyway, you oaf?'

'Nehesy's in the animal house,' said the man, his hand straying to scratch a carbuncle on the back of his neck.

'Fetch him,' said Huy, hoping he was not overdoing his act. The man started grudgingly on his errand. 'Wait.'

'Yes?'

'Who have they just taken away?'

'Isn't that in your book, Mr Organiser? That was Sherybin.'

'What was the guard for?' Huy thought back to the guard outside the audience chamber. That was less remarkable; but even so it was unusual to place a guard on a corpse.

'You tell me.'

'Going to the embalmers?'

The man nodded. 'High time. He's been in there four days.'

'Preparations had to be made.'

'I don't doubt that.' The man stood still, looking at Huy, scratching his collection of boils.

'What are you waiting for? Get Nehesy,' snapped Huy.

While he stood in the sun waiting, Huy rehearsed in his heart

42

what he would say. He had planned little for he would have to get the measure of the chief huntsman, and decide whether he was likely to be a friend or an enemy.

Wisely or not, he liked the look of the giant who came to meet him. Nehesy was a great wolf, as heavily built as Huy and about the same age, but nearly twice his size, so that he carried his weight better. He had open, generous eyes and a large nose and mouth, his big features making him seem larger than he was. At the moment he regarded Huy with curiosity mingled with irritation. Here was a man clearly unused to being summoned, and Huy could see by his expression that he had a certain opinion of indoor palace officials, particularly if they did not appear to outrank him. But how worried was he about his own future? Had not he been in charge of the fatal hunting party?

They saluted each other formally.

'Something about the dogs?' said Nehesy.

'Yes.'

'What about them?'

'Can we talk out of the sun?'

'Not used to it, are you?'

'How can you say that to a Blacklander?'

Nehesy looked taken aback, and then, to Huy's surprise, he smiled. 'Come on. I'm feeding them. Always like to do that myself. Anyway they know me; wouldn't take food from anyone else.' He turned without another word and led the way back to the cedar shed.

Its high roof made it cool, and the wind which constantly blew from the north kept it ventilated for the animals inside. Seven dogs, lithe tan-and-white creatures with silky ears, long snouts and feathered tails, paced their large enclosure, running up to the wooden rail and yelping plaintively when they saw Nehesy. From a large bucket made of sycamore wood which stood on the ground near the gate of the pen, he drew several handfuls of meat already cut into generous chunks and dropped them into a trough on the other side.

'Antelope,' he said. 'It's the cleanest meat, and it's all I'll give them. Now, what do you really want?'

Huy paused for a moment before replying. 'I'm conducting an inquiry about the accident. Just routine, for the palace records, but I couldn't tell your man because it is confidential.'

'Even he thought it was a bit early to be signing up the dogs for the king's procession to the tomb,' said Nehesy sombrely. 'And he isn't any brighter than a horse.' He finished ladling meat into the trough. 'What can I tell you that I haven't said already?'

'Whom did you report to?'

'Don't you know?'

'Tell me again.'

Nehesy hesitated. 'Horemheb.'

'Why?'

Nehesy would not meet his eye. 'You know how things are,' he said. 'I didn't want to get the blame for what happened.'

'What did happen exactly?'

'Haven't you seen the account I gave?'

'I'm gathering information for the palace,' said Huy. 'It's an independent inquiry. Nothing to do with Horemheb.'

Nehesy's eyes became more wary. 'Is it? I see . . . Well, I'd do anything in the world to help the queen, poor creature.'

As long as it does not cost you your neck, thought Huy, though he continued to smile. 'Keep our meeting to yourself,' he said, 'and there won't be any trouble.'

Nehesy nodded. The big man was as well aware as anyone that you did not leave it to the protector gods to watch your back.

'We awoke just before dawn,' he said. 'The cook had stoked up the fire and the water was on to boil for the *ful*. Apart from him, I was the first one up. I noticed the king's tent was closed; but then I saw that his chariot was gone. I felt Set's talons round my heart then, I can tell you.' He broke off, looking into Huy's face. The dogs had made short work of the meat but as he lingered by their enclosure they stayed near, looking up at him with hopeful yellow eyes.

'I ran to Sherybin's tent and of course he had gone, too. Then the guard who'd been on duty last came up and told me that one of the trackers had arrived back in camp an hour before the others, with news of wild cattle. Sherybin had set off with him and the king soon after.'

'What did you do?'

'I was furious at first. The trackers should report to me, not to the charioteers. But I knew the king would have been off after any worthwhile prey. It'd been a bad hunt, and wild cattle at this time of year are almost unheard of.' He paused, spread his hands. 'I roused the camp. We kicked out the fire and got the chariots ready. I only left two men to guard the tents. The rest of us set off after the king.'

'Was it light?'

'The sun was just coming up. We went as fast as we could, but we didn't call out to them. If they'd really found cattle we didn't want to spoil the hunt. Then we saw the chariot ahead of us.' Nehesy broke off, shuddering at the memory. 'I thought, that's my job buggered. But I feared for the king, too,' he added quickly, catching Huy's expression.

'I don't know how it could have happened, anyway,' he continued. 'It was in open desert, and Sherybin's one of the best drivers I've ever known. Maybe a rein snapped, or some other piece of tack broke. Must have done, because we found the horses not far away. They were panicky, but there wasn't a mark on them. Worst of all was the chariot. It was a new one, heavier to make it more stable, but something must have happened to turn it over. Poor Sherybin . . . if you could have seen him. Did you hear what happened?'

'Yes.'

'The king was lying a short way off, face down. His arms were spread out as if he was embracing Geb.'

'How had he died?'

'The back of the skull was smashed in.'

Huy was silent for a moment, trying to visualise the scene. But the only pictures his heart brought to him were of the wind swirling the sand into lonely, wild spirals in an empty grey void.

'Not even the trackers could find any trace of the cattle they were supposed to be after,' said Nehesy.

'What about the one who'd found them in the first place? Had he come back?'

'No one's seen him since.'

'How long had he been with you?'

'I don't know. Half a year, perhaps. But you know these country people. He probably saw the accident, got frightened, and ran off into the desert. You can live out there indefinitely if you know how. My guess is that he joined a ship bound for Punt. It's happened before, when people get scared enough.'

'And Sherybin?'

Nehesy thought. 'At least a year. He was young, but he was a good charioteer. That is why I let him drive the king.'

'They got on well?'

'They were like brothers.'

The dogs had lost interest in their master now, and had gone to lie down around the edges of their pen. Two rested their heads on their paws. The others still kept a watchful eye, between yawns.

'Where is the chariot now?' asked Huy.

Nehesy looked at him in surprise. 'Horemheb kept it.'

Huy looked at him. 'But not the horses?'

'No; they are back in the stables here.'

'How did he react to your story?'

'He was satisfied.' Nehesy said this challengingly, as if Huy should take warning from it.

'May I see the horses?'

Nehesy spread his hands. 'Of course.'

They walked out of the animal house and into the bright sunlight. The steeds were quiet now, standing in the scant shade afforded by the palm trees planted for the purpose in their corral. Nehesy undid the gate and led Huy towards them. At the smell of an approaching stranger, they stamped uneasily, and one flattened its ears; but Nehesy's presence reassured them.

'Which did he drive?' asked Huy.

'These two,' replied the huntsman, stroking the necks of a pair of sturdy animals which stood side by side. Huy, a townsman by nature and inclination, had not had much to do with horses, but the expensive and exotic beasts fascinated him. He approached them shyly, delighted by their gentleness, and the friendliness with which they responded to the touch of his hand. He looked carefully over their flanks and their trembling thighs, where on one a muscle twitched. Their tails flicked restlessly at angrily buzzing flies. There was not a mark on either horse.

Huy straightened. 'I don't know anything about these animals,' he said. 'But if the harness had snapped — if the chariot had overturned while they were still in the traces, mightn't there have been some breaking of the skin, or at least a burn mark?'

Nehesy looked at him.

Much later Huy sat in the sun, tired, letting its heat warm him like a lizard. Immobile as one, he let his heart sort out the events of the day.

It had not all been as successful as his meeting with Nehesy. The huntsman, believing him to be performing some kind of official duty, had indicated where he could find the chariot, but had not mentioned that it was impounded. From the guards Huy learnt that this was so because there would be a judicial inquiry into the death, and on asking what the origin of the inquiry was, was not surprised to hear that it stemmed from Horemheb's office. In itself that was not unusual, Huy told himself; but he was more determined than ever to look at the chariot.

As he had suspected, he could find no way to see either body. Both by now were in the initial stages of embalming, and he knew that they would be covered in the white natron salt which dried them, taking out the oil and water which in life fuel a man, but which in death rot him. The Medjay guard which was placed around the stable within the royal complex at the palace where the chariot was kept, and also the embalmers' shed, seemed heavier than Huy thought necessary, but under Horemheb the Black Land had become a place where the leaders' strength made itself felt. In the scant years of the reign of Tutankhamun, the old power of the king, which was absolute, but remote and benign, like the sun, had been replaced by something unsure of itself, less godlike; a power that needed to stress its presence by shows of force, by creating an unvoiced threat to any who would question it. If Akhenaten had broken the shackles by which the gods held the people in thrall, Huy thought, he had also sacrificed their innocence. By encouraging man to think for himself, he had obliged leaders to forge more terrible chains from now on, to control their subjects. A pessimist might think that only Ay's presence had reined in Horemheb's great ambitions; but perhaps Ay's own ambition had grown beyond its natural bounds as he, born a commoner, saw the Golden Chair as a closer possibility.

Huy had talked to the guards and parted from them on friendly terms, leaving the way open to another approach after his next interview with Ay. Dissatisfied as he was with the means of communication Ay had laid down between them, he awaited the arrival of the old man's messenger with impatience. But it seemed that Ay was as eager for contact as he was, for his man arrived shortly before dusk, looking furtive, and thus drawing attention to himself, as those do who are thrust without experience into undercover activity. He was a small, sleek man of thirty, with a fat belly, soft shoulders, and a finely oiled and plaited goatee. His black eyes were mistrustful and nervous, and he constantly moistened his lower lip with his tongue.

'Were you watching for me?' he asked as Huy opened the door to him.

'Yes.'

The man's eyes became even more cautious. 'Why?'

Huy shrugged. 'I was expecting you.'

'You didn't notice anyone following me?'

'If there was, I didn't see him. But he wouldn't come into the square. He would stay in the cover of one of the streets and see which house you came to from there.' Huy was amused. The man seemed to shrink into himself.

'Do they still follow you?'

'Who?'

The man made a gesture of impatience. 'The Medjays.'

'Well, I would have thought you'd know more about that than me.'

'I work for Ay, not Horemheb,' replied the man, with more strength of feeling than he had meant to reveal, for seeing Huy's expression, he moderated his tone, and added, 'Normally my work is confined to domestic duties, you see. I am unused to this. My name is Ineny.'

'May the Sun warm you and the River refresh you.'

The formal greeting pleased Ineny, who relaxed.

'Do not worry,' Huy continued. 'It is a long time since the Medjays lost interest in me. I have done little to attract their attention and I suspect that I am thought to be a danger to the state no longer. I imagine that Ay knows this. Of course I shall have to be discreet now.'

'Yes.'

'Do you bring a message for me?' Huy asked, fetching bread and beer. Ineny drank deeply before replying, looking grateful.

'No. Ay sent me for a report.'

'How much does he expect me to have found out so soon?'

'You have a certain reputation, it seems,' said Ineny, not without edge.

'There is little to tell yet, but I seek another meeting with your master.'

Ineny was doubtful. 'I am not sure about that. He wants

49

direct contact with you kept to a minimum. I came to you from my house, for example. He gave me a story to tell if I were stopped. That I was consulting you on a matter of my own.'

'Well, that is quite cunning. But I still need to see him.'

'I will have to ask. Can't I –?'

'No. I need to talk to him directly. Tell him that from what I have learnt it will not be possible to perform his task unless I have his close co-operation.'

Ineny looked unhappy. 'You want me to tell him that?'

'Yes. Do not worry, Ineny. It is my insubordination, not yours.'

'The messenger is blamed for the news he brings.'

'All jobs carry their risk.'

Ineny drank more red beer. 'And you have nothing you can tell me for him now?'

'No.'

Ineny had to be satisfied with that and left soon after. Once Ay's messenger was out of the way, Huy departed himself, and set off through the darkening streets on the long walk to the huntsmen's compound and the stables at the palace.

Nehesy's heart had begun to work on the possibility that the king might not have died by accident, and he was eager to help.

'But you must be discreet,' Huy warned him. 'Not a word of this to anyone. I am working on the direct orders of the queen, and if my inquiry ceased to be secret – well, I needn't tell you what the consequences would be, either for us or her.' Huy hoped that sounded portentous enough to impress the countryman.

'I want to find out what happened. I won't do anything that'll get in the way of that.' Nehesy's dignity made Huy ashamed of treating him like a hick.

They left before dawn, aiming to return soon after first light, before Nehesy would be missed, though as it was the Tenth Day – the Day of Rest – it was unlikely that the huntsman's absence would be noticed at all. The animals would not lack him, for the grooms would give them their morning feed. The dogs, as Nehesy explained with solicitude, were only fed once daily, in the afternoon.

They travelled alone, taking Nehesy's chariot, an old one, made of acacia wood with a sycamore axle bound in bronze and bronze fittings. Nehesy harnessed a pair of horses to the shaft, and released two of the dogs, Pepi and Ypu, from the pen. They darted out with whines of pleasure at this favouritism, while their fellows rose from sleep and loped a few paces before settling down again. Nehesy rubbed their noses and caressed them under the chin.

'Won't they be missed?' asked Huy.

Nehesy looked at him. 'By the great god,' he said, 'I wouldn't have your job. What must it be like, looking over your shoulder all the time? I've told my wife that I'm taking out a private hunter – we're not supposed to, but it's my rest day, and from time to time I let my staff do the same thing – a little extra funds, and quite a few of the palace officials are good customers. And there's something else too.'

'Yes?'

Nehesy looked at him, his big wolf's face opening in a generous grin. 'It's not something I expect you to believe, but there are no spies here.'

Regretting it in his heart, Huy indeed did not believe him.

The huntsman trundled the chariot out of the compound, the dogs scampering on ahead, looking and running back before darting ahead again, checking that they were on the course intended by their master, for though the palace owned them, they were Nehesy's animals.

As soon as they were free of the city, they gathered speed. Nehesy showed Huy how to jam his foot under the leather strap fixed to the floor of the chariot, to give him greater stability as they flew across the firm sand, heading south. The dogs, sure of their route now, had run away out of sight.

Unused to this form of transport, Huy braced his feet and

51

grasped the handhold at the front, trying to relax his knees at the occasional impact as the wheels found ripples shaped by the wind in the sand. He felt the breeze in his face and watched the backs of the horses' heads as they rose and fell, manes streaming. Below them, the ground, grey in the moonlight, was a blur. They continued to rush forward at a speed which seemed to Huy to increase until they were going so fast that he could hardly draw breath. Then Nehesy hauled on the reins, clicking at the horses. They slowed immediately, turning in a broad half-circle before coming to a halt at a place where the remains of a fire were still visible.

'This is where we camped,' said Nehesy. 'You can see the stones we gathered to hold down the corners of the tents.' He pointed at a number of small cairns set at regular intervals from one another. In four larger piles at the centres of these groups of cairns the tent poles must have been placed.

'The openings faced north?' asked Huy.

'They always do, to catch the wind.'

'So no one could have watched the king ride off, and then followed him?'

'Everyone except the king and Sherybin, and that one tracker, was here when we set off after them.'

Huy climbed down. The hard, bright moonlight threw the piles of stone into sharp relief. The chariot stood in the centre of the abandoned camp like a thing from a dream. The horses kept their heads up, alert, and the dogs appeared on the edge of the darkness, keen, eyes flashing silver, their spirits halfway back to their wild ancestors. A lizard scampered under one of the little cairns, and near Huy's foot a small area of sand heaved and subsided as something below burrowed deeper, sensing danger.

'Did you use this place many times?' he asked Nehesy, his voice sounding loud and coarse in the velvet darkness.

'In the season, once or twice a month.'

'And just as often recently?'

'Less so.'

That explained the desolate atmosphere. Unless there was a ghost here. Huy looked at Nehesy but he seemed unmoved by any other presence. Nor were the animals distressed. Perhaps being in the open at night, at this time just before dawn when the legions of Set were at their most powerful, when most men died and when most men were born, when the king under the earth was preparing for his rebirth, all his power drawn into himself – perhaps that was all it was.

But the feeling did not desert Huy as he climbed back into the chariot.

'Take me to where you found him,' he said.

The huntsman turned the chariot again and they headed further south, at a gentler speed this time. As they rode, the sun rose over a great emptiness. Away to the east were low hills, and immediately in front of them a clump of palms showed the location of a small oasis. Otherwise there was nothing, though the horses paced their course as if they were on a road.

They continued for an hour before Nehesy came to a halt.

'It was here,' he said.

Huy looked around. As far as he could see there was nothing to indicate that the place where they had stopped was different from any other they had passed, or which might have been to come. It crossed Huy's heart that if a trap had been laid to shut him up, then he had walked straight into it. Had he trusted Nehesy too easily? If the years spent in his new profession had taught him nothing else, it was to trust the most open people least.

'How do you know?' he asked, looking about him, but not descending from the chariot. Against his back, stuck into the waistband of his kilt under his cloak, he could feel the horn haft of his knife. Whether he would be able to defend himself against Nehesy he did not know.

'I left a marker.' Nehesy leapt from the chariot and walked over to where a javelin was stuck in the ground. 'The wind's blown all the tracks away – it had done that by the time we got here the first time – but I wanted to be sure I'd know the place again.'

'Had you intended to come back yourself?'

Nehesy paused. 'I don't know. I thought it might be useful.'

'It was,' said Huy, climbing down himself. 'Did anyone see you leave the javelin?'

'I didn't do it secretly, but there was a lot of activity. We were all in a panic. Our hearts had been taken over by the gods.'

'Where are the king's weapons?'

'At the palace.'

'Do you remember where you found the body lying?'

Nehesy walked and pointed. 'The chariot was here. The horses stood over there. A good way: fifty or seventy paces. Sherybin was hanging over the edge of the chariot, cut by a wheel.' He pointed again. 'And the king lay there.'

'I see.' Huy walked round to the chariot they had come on, and ran his thumb along the bronze-bound rim of one of its wheels. 'This is too thick to cut a man.'

Nehesy shook his head. 'This machine is old. The new ones are much faster, and the wheels thinner, made of metal.' He stamped on the sand. 'In the dry season, except for a thin covering, most of the desert is hard like a road here. There would be little danger of the wheels sinking in.'

'And the king's wound?'

'I told you. His head was smashed in at the back.'

'But how?'

Nehesy was exasperated. 'I don't understand you.'

'What smashed it? It can't have been a rock. There are none here.'

Nehesy looked around, his expression clearing. 'No . . .'

'Then what happened? Could he have struck it on some part of the chariot as he was thrown clear, or was he hit by a horse's hoof?'

'It's possible. But a horse is unlikely, because if they'd still been in the shaft, the chariot wouldn't have capsized.'

'And if he'd struck the chariot itself?'

'It's possible,' repeated Nehesy, but he looked doubtful again.

'Why is it unlikely? What is it?'

Nehesy shook his head. 'He must have hit the shaft somehow – or perhaps the hub of one of the wheels.'

'Why only that?'

'Because the body of the chariot is made of electrum – it's very light. If a man's head – or a block of wood or stone – anything hard – were to hit it, it would dent and cave in.'

Huy was silent. Somehow, he had to see the chariot. But doubts were turning into certainties now.

The dogs were specks on the desert, two hundred paces away, near the low rise of a dune. They would not respond when Nehesy called them.

'Let's go,' said the huntsman. 'If they won't come, they've found something.'

They mounted the chariot and drove the short distance. As they came to a halt once more, the horses shook their heads uneasily.

There would have been more of a stink if it had not been for the drying quality of the sand. As it was, the usual sweet stench, which filled your mouth and nostrils like foul rags, driving its long fingers down your throat and into your stomach, was replaced by a strong, musky odour. The dogs had not uncovered much yet – the meat was too bad for them to eat and in any case they were well enough trained to see that this was no food for them. From beneath the sand an arm rose, the fingers crooked except the index, which pointed towards the sky. Nehesy fetched a wooden spade from the chariot, strapped there to dig out bogged wheels, and began to clear away the soft sand of the dune.

The man was a husk – skin dried, eyes gone, mouth open. In the cavities, cleaner beetles were busily at work. He might have been caught in the act of swimming, the raised arm reaching diagonally back from his shoulder. Nehesy scraped away further, while the dogs watched with detached, intelligent interest. The hair of the corpse was dark and choked with sand, a forest in which small creatures crept. It stared at them forlornly from its eyeless orbits.

There was an untidy wound in his ribcage near his heart – someone had slashed at him from horseback. In his other hand he grasped a small linen bag. Huy took it and opened it. It contained five *kite*.

'A hard fee to resist,' said Huy. 'Your tracker?'

'Yes. But why leave him here?'

'There probably wasn't time to take him with them. How would they have done it? A quick burial. It's far enough away. No one would have expected anyone to come up here again within days – and with dogs.'

'But why kill him?'

'That's another question,' said Huy. 'Maybe he changed his mind, decided to try to warn the king. Perhaps there was a panic. Perhaps they never intended to let him live.'

'And why leave the money?'

'He'd earned his fee. Take it back, and his *Ka* would have sent a ghost after it.'

Nehesy nodded.

They reburied the remains of the tracker, as deep as they could, and Nehesy left the wooden shovel stuck in the mound above him as a marker. Huy recited what protecting words he could remember from *The Book of the Dead*:

'I am yesterday and I know tomorrow.
I am able to be born a second time . . .
I rise up as a great hawk going out of its egg.
I fly away as a hawk whose back is four paces long . . .
I am the snake, the son of the earth, multiplying
The years I lay myself down, and am brought forth every
    day.
I am the snake, the son of the earth, at the ends
Of the earth. I lay myself down and am brought forth

Fresh, renewed, grown young again every day . . .
I am the crocodile presiding over fear.
I am the god-crocodile at the arrival of his soul among the
   shades.
I am the god-crocodile brought in for destruction.'

The sun was already above the distant hills. They climbed into
the chariot and returned to the city.

# FIVE

Huy was standing in a white room with a broad balcony facing north. It gave a view over the sullen rooftops of the city and, beyond them, the fragile green strip which defined the course of the River seemed to stretch to infinity. The cool wind blew on his face.

Apart from the white, the colours in the room were gold and pale blue, and they were used sparingly, decorating the tops of the columns and a frieze of stylised leaves and boughs which ran around the walls just below the ceiling. The furniture was simple in design, but it was all of blackwood decorated with gold leaf. There were two chairs, a couch and a low table. On the table, the wine jug and beakers were of gold, and near them a silver-gilt bowl contained expensive *depeh* fruit.

Awe mingled with amusement in Huy's heart. He had told Nehesy that he was working for the queen – a lie of convenience to get him what he wanted; and now that lie was about to be turned into truth. The slight creature sitting at the table, a brown slip of a girl not sixteen, dressed in a plain cream robe edged with silver, her dark hair adorned with a circlet of thin gold on the front of which the uræus reared, looked at him nervously. In the course of their conversation she had let her regal dignity slip as she had relaxed, unburdening herself of fear.

'Do you think it is a judgement upon us by the Aten?' she asked timidly.

'The Aten does not judge. It only exists passively, to be made use of by us. Just as a cat or a hawk has no power over us except that which exists in our hearts.'

'But we turned from it. We changed our names.'

'The king ceased to be the Living Image of Aten, and became the Living Image of Amun. If there are gods at all, I think they are above the tricks we play to stay alive.'

'But if there is no principle, what is the point of existence?'

'There has to be belief to fuel principle, or it has no point itself. And does existence need to be justified? You were — forgive me — both too young to have made up your minds.'

'Whatever the reason, it has cost me dear.'

'The most important thing now is to make sure the little god inside you does not come to harm.'

'Or goddess.'

'Quite,' replied Huy, pleased to see a revival of spirit.

'You may sit down if you wish,' said Ankhsenpaamun. She had been fortunate to inherit more of her mother's features than her father's, though his lips and high cheekbones had come down to her. Her eastern eyes were large and dark; mature and candid.

Huy, trembling at such informality in front of his queen, did so.

'You wonder why I sent for you.'

'Yes.'

'You have friends. A former friend, Taheb. The shipowner.'

'I remember her.'

'I am sure you do,' replied the queen, with the faintest hint of humour in her voice. 'I think you were close once.'

'Yes.'

'I want you to find out what happened to the king. It will be difficult for me to help you; but I can pay you. Only your work must be done secretly.'

Huy was silent for a moment. He asked himself whether he should tell her that he had already been engaged on similar terms by Ay. He wondered how much deeper the water would get.

'You have your own resources.'

She made a gesture of impatience. 'I can trust very few people. Even when my lord was alive we were virtual prisoners here.

And that is the other thing I want you to look after: my safety.'

'Is there any reason to think you are in danger?'

She looked at him. 'Do not play the fool to draw me out. I carry the succession in my birth-cave. I carry that which will thwart the ambitions of Horemheb and my grandfather. The only difference between them is that Ay might not kill me, though he would not baulk at drowning the child.'

'I had heard that your grandfather had other plans.'

Her mouth curved in a bitter smile. 'To marry me? That would not save my child; he would try to get one of his own on me. But I doubt if he will dare propose marriage in the face of Horemheb. He would have to destroy the general first, and I am not sure that he has that much power.' She paused a moment, looking inside her heart. 'But on the other hand Horemheb has declared his ambition by marrying my aunt. The race for the succession has started.'

'Are you a competitor?'

'You are a clever man, Huy. But I know how hollow the feeling is when you sit on the Golden Chair. My ambition is humbler: it is to survive. One day, perhaps, Ay and Horemheb will destroy each other. Then there will be a place for my child. But the first thing is to make sure it lives to see that day.'

She looked at him again, childish uncertainty creeping behind the sophistication in her eyes. 'I have already been too frank. But you have to start trusting somewhere.' She paused, still hesitating, and bit her lip. 'There is a plan. You cannot be a party to it. Even before my husband was killed his successor had been selected.'

'Who is he?'

'Prince Zannanzash.'

'Of the Hittites?'

'Yes.'

'Why?' Huy found it hard to conceal his consternation.

'Their armies threaten us. The marriage would mean unity.'

'But who would control the Black Land? Would you be pharaoh, or consort?'

'He would be consort.'

Huy hesitated before replying. 'How far is this plan advanced?'

'I have sent a messenger to him. Soon he will set out for the Southern Capital.'

'With an army?'

'With an escort. He will come in peace. I do this for my dead husband. He wished to ensure peace in the Black Land. To block my grandfather and Horemheb.'

For how long, thought Huy, but said nothing. Instead, storing the knowledge up, and wondering who else had it, he decided on a different tack. 'Have you seen Nezemmut since her wedding? Talked to her?'

'No. She lived so long under my mother's shadow that she was a woman before her sun rose. Now she has her moment of glory in the face of Ra. I am an uncomfortable reminder of her past.'

Huy, bowing first, drank wine. He sank his head on his chest. 'I want to help you,' he said.

'There was a time when I could command. Now I must ask. But if a time of power came again – ' She broke off.

'I want to help you,' repeated Huy, formally. 'But I must tell you that I already have a commission in this matter.'

She looked at him, and her expression contained fear, anger, defiance and hope.

'Ay has already asked me to find out what happened.'

'Has he?' Her voice gave nothing away; but it did not save him from the candour of her eyes.

Huy told her what he had already found out, keeping back only those details which might injure her. He left the palace at nightfall, glad that the protagonists in the drama where he played a small role were too busy watching each other to pay much attention to him.

Meanwhile, Ineny had done his work well, and arranged an

61

interview with Ay. The old man did not begrudge this. He struck Huy as one who would do anything without complaint, even to the injury of his self-esteem, if it furthered his ambition. He reminded the scribe of those people who keep the rudder of their life-ship under a firm hand, always looking towards a distant but fixed goal. At the age of twenty they know what they wish to have achieved by fifty. They set sail, and in due time they arrive at the distant port. Huy did not know whether such people were to be envied or pitied.

'I need to talk to the doctors who examined him.'

Ay's expression did not change. 'Why? Is there doubt that it was an accident?'

'There is some.'

Now the old man looked at him keenly. 'What doubt?'

'I am collecting information. But I must speak to the doctors if I am to give you a case.'

'The doctors may be Horemheb's men.'

'Horemheb is not so powerful that he has everybody in his pocket. He cannot yet do precisely as he pleases.'

These words gratified Ay. 'That is true. It is as bad to overestimate as to underestimate,' he said. Huy wondered what the old man's assessment of him was. He knew that he was involved in what was, for him, a dangerous game; but he was in no doubt of where his loyalties lay. He did not care for Ay or Horemheb, or anyone who took it that a country was merely an accessory of their own personality, an ornament for the overweening little god within them. He would have liked to see both these jockeying men devoured by crocodiles. But in truth, he knew that one of them would soon be pharaoh.

As he left, Ineny gave him the names of the two doctors. Both were high officials at the House of Healing, though twenty years separated them. The younger was in his twenties; the older, close to fifty. Huy decided to visit the younger man first.

Merinakhte was from the south. He had the tall, lean build of a desert dweller, a sour mouth and dry, professional eyes.

He received Huy in a low, dark room on the ground floor of the House of Healing. The weather had turned humid, and Huy, who suffered badly when the atmosphere was moist, was painfully aware of how much he was sweating in the heat. He was dressed in a plain kilt and a simple, light headdress, but nevertheless he could feel the water run from under his hair down his neck, and gather round his waist, trickling down his legs.

He was equally aware of the disdain with which Merinakhte regarded him. The young doctor did his best to disguise this, though his own arrogance and self regard would not let him succeed entirely. He remained dry and cool – bloodless as a lizard. Huy had no doubt that he deliberately interviewed people in this room, where the worst effects of the heat were intensified, to put them at a disadvantage from which he did not suffer himself.

'You come from Ay?'

'Indirectly. His office started the inquiry I am following up.'

Merinakhte frowned. 'But there is an official investigation into the king's death. I have told them all I found at the examination.'

'We are working in tandem with the official inquiry. A method of cross-checking our information,' lied Huy, praying that the doctor would not cross-check himself. It seemed unlikely. The man had climbed too high too young to be anything other than a political appointee, and as such he would be careful not to tread on the toes of any potential master. Even if Horemheb had put him where he was, he would still not feel confident enough to defy any emissary of Ay. Huy wondered how many people like Merinakhte there were in the Southern Capital now – little people who had climbed on to one or other of the emmer-carts of the two men now in contention for the Golden Chair. No voices, he reflected, had been raised on behalf of the unborn god-king beginning to form inside the queen. Even the gods of the city, massive and enigmatic in their solid temples, had remained discreetly silent.

'You were the first to see the king after his accident?' asked Huy.

'No. I only saw him after he was brought back to the city.'

'How long was it since his death when you saw him?'

'Not long at all. It was early morning still. They brought him directly here.'

'And what was the cause of death?'

'Surely you must know that,' snapped Merinakhte.

'I know what the wound was. How do you think it was caused?' replied Huy evenly.

'An accidental blow.'

'He must have been hit by something sharp and solid?'

'I don't know what it is you want me to say, but there is no question of its being anything other than an accident.' Merinakhte's voice was still aggressive, though an element of caution had crept in.

'Did you see the chariot?'

'Why would that have been necessary?'

Huy paused. 'Do you think, then, that he might have struck his head on part of the chariot, or its equipment, as he fell from it?'

'That is obvious. Really I do not see the point of this insulting cross-questioning. My reputation is a high one. How do you think I became a deputy-governor of the House of Healing?'

Huy spread his hands, deprecatingly. 'I merely follow orders,' he said in a manner designed to be irritating.

'Ask any of my colleagues. They will tell you the same.' Merinakhte became conciliatory. 'Ask Horaha. He conducted the examination with me.'

'I intend to.'

'Good.'

They glared at each other for a moment, Merinakhte still unsure. Huy could imagine the message speeding to Horemheb as soon as he had left. He wondered if the general would take any action, but felt moderately secure in his own unimportance. Merinakhte would describe him as 'a messenger purporting to come from Ay', or in similar terms. Horemheb would wonder at that, and get his spies to investigate further. Ay's household would be ready to confuse them.

'One last thing,' said Huy.

'Yes?'

'Whom did you report to?'

Merinakhte allowed himself a superior smile. 'Are you really from Ay? You seem remarkably ill informed. Do you have any written authorisation?'

'You're leaving it a little late to ask for that,' retorted Huy. 'The degree of your co-operation has been noted.' With that, he turned on his heel, inwardly content at the insecurity he had sown.

He left the House of Healing and made his way out of the main courtyard, turning right and heading towards the little compound set among *dom* palms where the doctors' houses were arranged in neat rows, separated by tidy gardens, each with its own containing wall and central fishpond. The shady streets which divided them were swept and clean, and mingled with the pleasing smell of dust and distant spices which hung over most of the city apart from the dirty, cluttered harbour quarter, there was the scent of safflowers.

The building he was looking for stood on its own at the end of a row, on a corner where two streets met. He knocked at a door painted a dull red, set into a white, plastered wall, over whose top oleander clambered, scattering it untidily with pale pink flowers.

The door was opened to him by a house servant who ushered him into a large garden and asked him to wait. The house, raised on a platform against possible flood from the River, which ran close by, was tall and white, and partly hidden behind the cypress tress which had been planted along the edge of the rectangular pool. Two gardeners were busy, one watering a large kitchen garden, the other, half hidden, thinning out an enormous bank of blue and yellow flowers which rose against the inner side of the street wall. The lattice windows of the main reception room were set high in the house, and above them rose the two vents to catch the north wind. It was a bigger place than most of the others in the compound. Huy noticed that the interior doorposts were set with lapis lazuli.

A pair of *ro* geese waddled over curiously from the direction of the pool to look at him. As they did so, their owner appeared in the doorway of the house.

Horaha came slowly across the garden to meet him, leaning heavily on a blackwood stick. He wore no headdress, and his bald head was bronzed by the sun. He was dressed in a calf-length pleated kilt and a short upper robe with half-sleeves, from which wiry arms projected, ending in hands that seemed too big for them, with long, agile fingers. A high wooden sole had been attached to the sandal he wore on the foot of his bad leg, which protruded, withered and thin, from below the hem of the kilt. Huy, having noticed it, quickly withdrew his gaze and did not look in its direction again. He had always been careful in matters of everyday courtesy.

The elderly doctor was not alone. Walking with him was a girl with the same intelligent face, but more delicate, subtle features. She had a clear, high forehead, framed by a mass of black hair dressed in a complex braid. Her large chestnut eyes were set under slender dark-brown eyebrows, and her fine nose above a generous mouth, curved in a smile which was partly defensive. Her chin was firm without being obstinate. She was tall – taller than Huy – and she had broad shoulders and full breasts, though her legs were long and slim, and her hips almost boyish.

Wooden folding chairs had been brought out from the shade of the house and set under a tamarisk tree, where house servants brought Dakhla wine, honey and figs. Horaha's manner was hospitable and charming; but he could not disguise an inner lack of ease.

'How private do you wish this interview to be?' he asked Huy. 'I have not introduced you to my daughter. She is Senseneb, and since my wife's death she has been my right hand – more. I have no secrets from her, and if anything she knows more about my affairs than I do myself.'

He was talking too much, too fulsomely; out of nervousness, Huy supposed. He smiled at the girl, but she did not relax her own expression. She would remain defensive until she knew whether or not he intended harm to her father.

'Are you a doctor too?' he asked her politely.

'My father has taught me,' she replied, non-committally.

'There is no reason for you not to stay, if you wish,' said Huy, and was pleased to see her expression unstiffen.

As their conversation progressed, Huy was happy to find that there was very little of the restraint that had surrounded his talk with Merinakhte. Or rather, the restraint was of a different kind. The unease he had been aware of in Horaha did not diminish, and though Senseneb said little she would occasionally dart her father a warning glance. To try to relax them more, Huy played the part of the bland bureaucrat, making routine enquiries for the record, given that the death in question concerned the most important person in the country. He affected a lack of interest in the question of the pharaoh's successor, taking the line that whoever ruled, people like him would always be needed. This act went some way towards having its desired effect, though despite himself Huy was sorry to see that Senseneb was beginning to look at him with mild contempt. A large and indolent cat, one of two that were prowling around the table, leapt on to his lap and settled there, purring.

He wondered how old Senseneb might be. Not a girl any more, she might have been at the end of her third decade. Had she been married? Was she still? Did she have children? Her face told him nothing, and Huy fought his curiosity. It was not relevant.

They had come to the cause of the king's death. Horaha exchanged more frequent glances with his daughter, and even their posture began to betray the anxiety they felt. Huy could not ignore this.

'You tell me you believe Nebkheprure Tutankhamun died

accidentally,' he said. 'But your faces and your bodies tell me a different story.' He looked from one to the other, but neither would meet his eye. 'Do not be concerned that this conversation will be repeated farther than is necessary. It is the truth that we want.' Huy chose his words carefully. 'If you believe that the king died by someone's hand, do you not think that his *Ka* will not see you as accomplices if you do not speak of it?'

'Perhaps the Black Land has reached a point where the living great are more to be feared than the dead,' said Senseneb finally. Her father bowed his head. Huy realised that he had played his petty official role too well. They would never trust him with open hearts. But Senseneb had already said too much.

'What do you mean?' he asked her quickly.

Her eyes blazed at last. 'I mean that there is little room for truth.'

Horaha raised his hand too late to stop her speaking. Now he let it fall.

'You had better tell me what you think,' Huy said to him, but without threat in his voice. He wished he could be honest with this man, and tell him that in truth he represented the interests of the queen. He knew without being told that they thought the king's death was no accident, and had sound reasons for that belief; but even if he were frank with them, would they believe him?

Huy told himself to be patient. Perhaps he could come back, once he had gathered more information, and lay it before them. Then they might exchange their knowledge for his, and he would have the foundations of a badly-needed alliance with which to help the queen. But for the moment he could not know, or risk too much intimacy. It was frustrating that a lack of trust kept him from knowing exactly what conclusions Horaha had drawn from his examination of the king; but perhaps it was as important to know that they existed. And unless they were past masters, both Horaha and his daughter were amateurs in the art of subterfuge. If he had not been on their side, they had already given him enough to destroy them.

'My father has told you all he can,' said Senseneb as she walked him to the gate. 'There is no doubt that the king's death was a tragic accident.'

'It leaves the queen badly exposed,' said Huy, deliberately dropping his guard at this unexpected opportunity.

'But that is simply the will of the gods,' she replied, looking at him. 'Wouldn't you say?'

'If Tutankhamun's death was an accident, yes.'

She looked at him more closely. 'Do *you* think otherwise?'

Huy did not answer. Senseneb's expression changed, and he knew that she was wondering whether her first assessment of him was correct. He left her with the question in her mind, still unsure if the seeds of an alliance were here. His main concern was that he had impulsively laid himself open to betrayal. But he could not see Senseneb or her father as servants of Horemheb. And he hoped that they would not be left with the impression that he was.

It was late when he left the beautiful house in the doctors' compound. What a perfect place it seemed, and yet how sad and confused were its occupants. Huy, thrust out of the quiet and secure life he had trained for, which was all he had ever wanted, had come with time to know that such a life does not exist. In such a house, in such a garden, he might still have believed it possible. But he knew that in the end the only quiet place, the only cool pool beside which he could sit in total security, was the one buried at the centre of his heart.

Unfortunately walls were not enough to shut out life.

He made his way under the lengthening shadows of the sycamores and acacias down through the town towards the harbour quarter, but he did not go home immediately. Instead, he headed for the string of eating houses which ran along the quay where the broad-bottomed bullion barges were tied up. A scattered light from their frontage was thrown against the implacable darkness which was gathering over the River. Very faintly, through the haze, the fires of the workmen engaged in their never-ending task of tomb excavation glowed on the West Bank.

Huy wondered how work on Tutankhamun's hastily-prepared grave was progressing. He had heard that it was nearing completion. The burial would take place as soon as the body was ready, Ay's messenger Ineny had told him. All the arrangements had been taken over by Ay, but no agreement had yet been reached over who should perform the rite of Opening the Mouth.

The smell of linseed oil, *bak*, and spices reached his nostrils as he approached the untidy line of buildings open at the front, with small tables sprawling out onto the quayside as far as the lantern light would reach.

A number of diners sat at each establishment. They were mainly rivermen, and the noise of the conversation and the mingled smells of cooking, the scurrying of the serving men and girls, and the steam and smoke from the fires and the clay ovens at the rear, created a chaotic and amiable inferno in which it was easy to hide. Threading his way through tables Huy found Nehesy seated near the back of the third eating house, an untouched bowl of duck and lentils in front of him, his hands clasping and unclasping impatiently. He half rose as Huy quickly sat next to him, placing a hand on his arm.

'No one saw you arrive?' asked Huy.

'They don't know my face down here, or I'd have been mobbed. Everyone's talking about the king's death. I overheard more than one bargemaster say he wasn't continuing on to the Northern Capital until he was sure who the next pharaoh was going to be.'

'It won't make any difference to them.'

'It won't make any difference to most of us; but we like to think it's important that we know.'

Huy smiled. 'Maybe we're being optimistic to think that it won't make any difference. Did you see the chariot?'

Nehesy glanced around quickly. 'Yes. The guards weren't too happy about it at first, but as soon as I told them who I was, they let me in. Especially as I happened to take along a couple of antelope hides, which they were very happy to accept.'

'What did you tell them?'

'That I needed to check the equipment – the sand shovel, what weapons were left – for my own report.'

'And?'

Nehesy leant forward. He thrust his great head forward, placed his elbows on the table, and spread his hands wide. 'In the confusion when we found the king and brought him back, I didn't take in much detail, but I can tell you this now: the chariot is completely undamaged. There isn't a dent on its shell. I don't know if they've cleaned it – it doesn't look like it because there's still plenty of sand caught in the axle and around the wheel spokes – but there isn't a trace of any blood, or hair, or skin. I *saw* the wound on the king's skull. If he had struck it on the chariot there would be signs of where he got the blow.'

'You're sure it would have dented the shell?'

Nehesy spread his hands wider in impatience. 'Look, those electrum chariots are feather light. The metal would bend if you blew on it. There is something else too.'

'Yes?'

'The harness has disappeared. All of it. Bridle, bit, reins, girth – all gone. The guards knew nothing of it, and it wasn't returned to the stables.'

Huy paused for a moment, thinking. Then he said, 'What will happen to the chariot?'

'The story is that it will be buried with the king. The new officer in charge of the official inquiry has inspected it.'

'Then there is nothing we can do,' said Huy.

'You can tell Ay what we've found out. What did the doctors say?'

Huy told him.

'Then there is enough to go on. With that information, if Ay cannot block Horemheb . . .' Nehesy broke off in exasperation, as Huy continued to hesitate.

71

'We can't assume Horemheb is responsible for the king's death,' Huy said, finally. 'He's not the only one who stands likely to profit by it, and if he has no other virtue, he has shown himself to have patience.'

'Consider this then,' said Nehesy. 'The man in charge of the inquiry is Kenamun. He is the new chief of police.'

Huy drew in his breath. He thought of the unsettled score he had with the former priest-administrator. In those days Kenamun had been Horemheb's man; there was no reason to think that things had changed.

He did not notice a boatman at the next table rise and leave, his plate of food untouched.

# SIX

As soon as she awoke she knew something was wrong. At first she lay still, trying to guess by the quality of the light what time it was. From the cold and the stillness, she knew that morning was still far away. Then she wondered what it was that had awakened her so suddenly, so absolutely. All that was left in her heart was the memory of a noise, or of the ceasing of a noise.

She was not frightened. She lay and looked at the window, framing white moonlight. Some spilled into the room, and she waited until her eyes grew into it enough for her to see her way without a lamp. When she was satisfied, she threw off the sheet and stood up, naked in the cool darkness, enjoying the sensation for a moment before she directed her attention to the silence around her; the noise of the sheet and the creaking of the leather bedstraps had been an intrusion, and now it had returned, more intense than before.

Suddenly she realised what had awakened her: the coughing had stopped. She pulled on her long robe and left the room, walking briskly along the verandah, open on one side to the sky, to her father's room.

The house servant whose bed was placed outside it was already awake, and unable to decide what to do. Pushing him aside, Senseneb grabbed the handle of the door and opened it.

Horaha lay on his back, his neck reposing on a bone headrest, the oil lamp beside him still burning. His arms were splayed, his hands open, palms upwards. His head had fallen back and his lips and eyes were open. His body was still. The only movement was from the minute bubbles that frothed and broke at the corners of his mouth.

'Get Hapu,' she told the servant at her elbow, but even as he ran to fetch the chief steward she knew that her father was dead. She had probably known it the moment she had entered the room and seen him. A large yellow moth which had been fluttering around the lamp now left its rotating course and settled near Horaha's eye. For a second Senseneb found herself hoping to see the cheek flinch, but the moth might as well have landed on a statue.

She was astounded at how calm she felt. She crossed the room to the body and checked pulse and breath as he had taught her, automatically, seeking refuge from her feelings, keeping them at bay through the actions she took. Soon enough the thoughts would pour in. She was an orphan and a divorcee, with no children and no other relatives. Though she knew enough to practise medicine, it would be hard here in the Southern Capital. She would have to go away, but where?

She pushed the door of her heart closed. For the moment it would be enough to find out what had happened.

There was a sound of running feet, bare feet on the wooden floor of the verandah. She turned to see Hapu, closely followed by the frightened house servant.

'What has happened?' the steward asked, scared himself.

'Horaha is dead. We must make his *Khat* comfortable,' she said. Her voice was firm. The commands that came from it calmed the men. They came into the room, glad to escape from the tumbling rush of their own feelings in activity.

'Do what is necessary,' she continued. 'We must send for the embalmer at dawn. But I want to speak to him before he touches the body.'

'Yes, Lady.'

She noticed the title they had instantly accorded her. Up until now, she had been Returned Daughter of the House. It was three years since her husband had divorced her on grounds of barrenness, and sent her back to her father. Her husband, a kind man, had even paid her the agreed divorce fund which had been settled at their marriage, and had not told her parents that he had other grounds for divorce: her adultery. Her mouth felt acid at the recollection. Seven wasted years. Why should she think of them now? Perhaps because she was alone again.

When they had done, removing the headrest and replacing it with a large pad of linen, then resting the arms on more linen pads, they went to fetch the linen sheet soaked in water in which they would cover the corpse to keep the insects away. Alone with her father, she leant close to his face and dabbed away the foam at his lips. It smelt rank.

She drew back, stood up, thinking. It was two days since that thickset investigator from Ay's household had been here. He had tried hard to play the little official, but his eyes were too intelligent and his mouth too humorous to deceive her. They had fenced with each other, but there had been something in the air between them which had made them sense each other as friends. Who was he really? She had little doubt that she would see him again, but how soon? It seemed that she needed him urgently, and she did not know where to find him.

In the stillness, she sent a thought to him, concentrating hard. If it reached him, he would come.

Two days. Who had betrayed her father? Perhaps Merinakhte. But her refusal to sleep with him was too small a reason for such vengeance. There was no doubt in her mind that Horaha had been poisoned.

When had the coughing started? Early the previous day. Horaha had put it down to a chill caught at the bank of the River during the Oblation to Hapy. The dry season was nearing its end and Horaha had been chosen as one of the officials to offer this year's sacrifice for the flood. He had drunk the holy river water, but so had all the others chosen. Horaha had taken no food or drink outside his own house since then that she had not taken too. Indeed, since the noon meal yesterday he had eaten nothing, taking only the herb tea he had prescribed himself. It seemed insane, she thought, that he had to die in the middle of the best community of doctors in the entire Black Land.

She knelt by her father, holding his hand, knowing that nearby two of the Eight Elements, his *Khou* and his *Ka*, would be standing in the gloom. His *Ba* would be preparing itself for the long lonely journey through the Twelve Halls. Struggling with her thoughts, she remained with Horaha until dawn, sending message after message to Huy. Perhaps it would work, though with the generations the Blacklanders were losing this gift of communication.

Then, shortly before dawn, she saw in her heart's eye a stocky figure leave a house in a shabby street in the harbour quarter, and she knew that he had heard her.

Huy's first thought was that the killing had been committed with such crude disregard for secrecy that it was meant to be taken as a warning.

'You will have to heed it,' he told Senseneb.

'How?'

'Keep your head down. Do nothing.'

'How can I do nothing?' she asked angrily. 'Anyway, they will be watching the house. They will have seen you come.'

'That is not unnatural. You did not summon me by any means they could track. As far as they are concerned, I was bound to come back here. If they are watching me – or you – at all.'

'They must want to know what has happened.'

'They will hear about it soon enough in any case.'

Senseneb was silent. Then she said, 'What is this all about?'

'A struggle for power,' replied Huy. 'Do not look so stern. Why do you not give in to your grief?'

'I am not ready yet,' she answered. 'I am not yet brave enough to face it.'

The embalmer came with his assistants and his long cart.

Soon the shell that had contained the Eight Elements of Horaha was taken away to be prepared for the spirit that would inhabit it eternally. They watched it go from the gate and turned back into the garden. Suddenly, her shoulders started to shake.

He held her as her body was racked with sobs. Nervous servants peered from windows and doorways, but Hapu brought water to wash her and wine to drink, and together he and Huy nursed her through the first wave of misery. Later, sitting up on the couch by the pool, the pet *ro* geese solicitously attending her, she looked at the former scribe with tired eyes and smiled.

'I will not apologise for my tears, but I am ashamed of some of the reasons for shedding them. I am alone now, and soon I will have nowhere to live.'

'What will happen to this place?'

'It belongs to the House of Healing. It is the residence of the chief doctor, and as soon as a new one is appointed, he will move in.'

'Where will you go?'

'My father owns a place far to the south, in Napata. It is a long way from the Southern Capital.'

'How long will they let you stay here?'

She sighed. 'At least until my father is in his tomb. The funeral rites must be controlled from here and they would not risk the anger of his *Ka*.'

'His killers risk that already.'

'I have never known the dead avenge themselves yet. Have you?'

'No.'

She sighed, stretched her long limbs, and looked at Huy with the ghost of a smile again. 'I am glad you caught my thought.'

'It was vivid. I was sleeping when it came and it woke me.'

'I did not think it would work.'

'There are few left who can use the air between us.'

'I could not do it again.'

'I hope you will not have to.'

Huy poured wine and they drank together. The sun was heading towards its zenith, warming the tamarisk's grey, awl-shaped leaves; but in its shade it was still cool, and the garden had trapped a breeze which touched their faces.

'Will you tell me now what Horaha believed happened?' Huy asked quietly, hoping he was not pushing too fast or too soon.

'Yes.' She sighed again, sipping the wine and drawing her legs up, encircling her knees with her arms. 'It is certain that the king died because of a blow to the head; but if he had been thrown from the chariot there would have been bruises on other parts of his body. My father thought that the only other explanation was that he might have been thrown clear and struck his head on a rock.'

'No,' said Huy. 'There are no rocks. And the king could not have been thrown clear, because he would have had one foot in the floorstrap of the chariot.'

Senseneb said, 'Then he was killed deliberately.'

'Yes.'

'That is what my father had begun to think.'

'I see.'

'Who did it?'

'I do not know.'

'Was it Horemheb?'

Huy sighed. 'Or Ay.'

'But Ay has hired you to find out the truth, hasn't he?'

Huy smiled. 'You think as an antelope runs.'

'What will you do with what you know?'

Huy was silent.

'But you must tell Ay,' continued Senseneb. 'He must be impatient for news from you.'

'I am expecting his messenger to come today.' Huy drank a cup of wine, and squinted up through the leaves at the sun.

'He would reward you well.'

'That is true. But then I would be in his debt.'

78

Senseneb looked at him. He was not the kind of man whom she would have thought attractive, but the eyes carried the face. She wanted to tell him about herself, to explain why she had been unfaithful to her husband, to tell him how certain she was that she could bear children. But why did she want to?

'Do you think your father was killed because of what he believed?'

'Yes,' she replied quietly.

'Who was with him at the Oblation to Hapy?'

She looked at him. 'His colleague Merinakhte, and Senefer, the High Priest of Amun. Horemheb and Ay, and the priests of Mut and Khons; and Horemheb's chief of police, Kenamun.'

After he had left her and made his way home again to await Ay's messenger, Huy thought about his own powerlessness to stop a chain of events which would lead to more deaths within the next days, or weeks at the latest. He was sure that, short of a miracle, a bloodbath would follow the burial of the king, and he knew that unless he acted very quickly, the net gathering round the queen would have so tightened that he would not be able to release her from it. He wondered what secret guard had been placed on her already; then he considered that perhaps it was too soon. The general might feel confident enough not to place a guard on her. For after all, what could she do to him?

Any last doubt about who was responsible for the king's death had vanished with Senseneb's news that Kenamun had been near her father close to the time of his death, despite the fact that Horemheb liked to show off his control of the powerful police at any and every public occasion — especially the corps now known in the city as the Black Medjays, created by Horemheb in the national interest, as he put it, but answerable only to him. The warning function of Horaha's demise was clearer than ever.

The problem which faced Huy was how much to tell Ay. He had looked at what he had learned, and he knew that in Ay's hands, it could be enough to bring Horemheb down. He acknowledged to himself that he was now in water so deep that his feet no longer touched the bottom. He was unsure what beasts might be swimming below the muddy surface, ready to seize his legs and drag him under. Ay had his own ambitions, and Huy was wary of underestimating so adept a survivor.

There was no way of avoiding a report to the Master of Horse. As the time for his interview with the old man approached, he went over the ground he had covered. What could he say, and what could he leave out? It seemed to him that he had three aims to serve: what was best for Queen Ankhsenpaamun; what was best for his own survival; and finally, what was best for the country.

The Black Land was in a deep crisis. Critically weakened by Akhenaten's neglect of its northern empire, now lost, the country was threatened by warring Syrian tribes and by the Hittites, now pressing forward from the north, from the lands beyond the Great Green. The army was concentrated in the Delta, since to the south the peoples of Napata and Meroe had remained loyal, taking no advantage of the collapse of power at the centre.

There was no concerted move against the empire yet, as the foreigners were content to bicker over and enjoy the territory they had so recently won, but sooner or later the Black Land would have to strike back, or be lost forever. If they lost control of the River . . .

An unpleasant conclusion had lodged in Huy's heart and grew there. Ay did not have the power or the personality to save the country. Horemheb did. Huy knew that the ultimate battle between the two men would not concern him, and he did not want to be involved in tipping the balance of power. But he was faced with the choice of backing one of two tyrants, and if the country were to be saved and survive, and he accepted that its survival overrode any other consideration, a choice had to be made. He wished the gods had not cast him in this role.

But there might be a way of using what he knew to buy the

queen's safety. After that, let Horemheb and Ay slog it out. He braced himself for the rough water ahead.

Ineny arrived to fetch him early. He was agitated, detached, and at first even less disposed to conversation than Huy.

'What is it?'

'Ay's losing patience,' replied Ineny, shortly.

'With me?'

'With the whole situation. Horemheb has practically taken over the entire investigation of the king's death, on the grounds that Ay has more important things to do.'

'What are they?'

'The funeral arrangements, of course. But who is going to preside at them?'

Huy wondered who was looking after the protection of the northern frontier; but he guessed that Horemheb would have most of the generals under his wing. Ineny had arrived in a large, covered litter almost too broad for the streets. The carriers had to step over three or four beggars who crouched in their usual spots by the side of buildings, and from outside the two men could hear curses as the litter lurched over.

'What do you think the end of this will be?' Huy asked Ineny.

'There are so many rumours inside the palace compound that you could weave a fishing net with them.'

'What about the official inquiry? Have they issued a statement yet?'

'No. But the news has broken of Horaha's death.'

'How has that been reported?'

'Natural causes.'

Huy was silent. No one could disprove that. Whatever poison had been used had left none of the telltale marks – blue lips, a rictus after death – and even if Senseneb could prove that her father had been killed, Huy doubted that she would be wise to try. The time for avenging her father would come, and it

81

would be in a way that did not put her fruitlessly in danger, he would see to that.

His thoughts turned to Kenamun. A picture of the long, bony face with its thin beard appeared in his heart's eye. Kenamun, the sadist, whose murder of the little Babylonian prostitute some years ago he had been powerless to prove. Kenamun, whose career under Horemheb's protection had never faltered, and never would while the general needed to dip his hands in blood.

'I know nothing of it,' said Huy. 'But the reason for the king's death must be given soon.'

'You know what it will be,' said Ineny.

The litter tilted again, and from the greater sunlight that shone through the linen curtains, Huy knew that they were out of the harbour quarter and had started to cross the open space which separated the city from the palace compound.

'Why do you live in that area?' asked Ineny, whom the conversation appeared to soothe. 'It stinks of fish, and all the people who aren't sailors are cut-throats.'

'You get used to it,' said Huy.

'That doesn't answer my question. You've got quite a reputation.'

'And I'll keep it by staying quiet. If I don't, I'll lose my living and my head.'

'You can't help getting known about,' said Ineny. 'Once you pass a certain stage, you can't help getting noticed. Even in a big place like this.'

Huy looked across at him. 'Are you telling me something, Ineny?'

'I just want to be on the winning side when all this is over.'

'That may be a long time yet.'

The massive wall of yellow stone towered above them as they climbed out of the litter by a side-gate of Ay's house. The gate was a cavernous rectangular portal set so deep in the wall that the carvings of its lintel were lost in shadow.

But as they approached, a small door set in the greater swung open soundlessly.

The court they stood in was brown and bare. The sandy floor had been swept, but not a plant grew to relieve the severity of the high walls which surrounded them. The only decoration was a massive statue of Ay. As always, he was shown young, an expression of impenetrable blandness on his face, to which the sculptor had given some of the features of Tutankhamun, in a further attempt to bolster Ay's claim to the throne. They crossed the gash of sunshine that slanted down in a precise rectangle defined by the building, and entered a doorway on the other side of the yard, at the entrance to which stood two Nubian guards in the white kilts and dark blue headdresses of Ay's livery.

Ay received them in the same room as before, but his manner was agitated and he did not sit at the low table by the balcony.

'You have been slower than I anticipated,' he said to Huy.

'It is not always possible to produce quick results, especially when they are of such importance.'

'Indeed. But you lag behind the official inquiry. No doubt you and Kenamun have been treading on each other's toes?'

'On the contrary, I have not seen him.'

Ay seemed to be weighing something in his heart. 'No – of course you would not. His inquiry did have a start on yours.'

'I have seen no evidence of his inquiry.'

'What have you found out for me?'

Huy had decided what to say, but framing the words took a moment.

'Come on,' said Ay, impatiently. 'I needn't tell you what rewards will be yours if you prove yourself useful to me.'

'What is your plan?' asked Huy.

Ay looked at him angrily. 'What do you mean?'

'Before I tell you what I know, I must see how you will use it.'

'What business is it of yours how I use it? I am interested in finding out the truth. The king was like a son to me.'

'And you mistrust Horemheb's inquiry?'

'We have been over this before. I told you, if you accepted the job, you had to accept my terms with it.'

'What I have found out may be too important for that.'

Ay narrowed his eyes. 'Then it wasn't an accident?'

'No.'

Ay looked away. 'Can you prove it?'

'Yes. But I must have time. There are still pieces missing.'

'If you can't find them we can manufacture them. What have you got so far?'

'I will not tell you.'

Ay looked at him. 'Be careful, Huy. You are playing a very dangerous game. What are you after? Do you intend to sell to the highest bidder? If that is so, let me tell you that you will not even leave here to make your sale.'

'I cannot tell you my plan; but you will not kill me either. You need what I can give you because it will bring Horemheb under your power.'

'You are very confident. Does it not strike you that you cannot leave this house without my permission? Why don't I give orders now to have the information tortured out of you?'

'Because I have no doubt that Horemheb knows where I am, and he will be intrigued. He is waiting for you to make your play. Keep me here, torture me, and you will alarm him into action before you are ready to defend yourself.'

Ay turned to look out over the river. It was beginning to fill with the red sand that heralded the flood.

'I can weave you a net strong enough to catch the general,' continued Huy. 'But if you want it to *be* strong enough, you must wait.'

'Of course you realise that you are speaking treason of one regent to another? Why don't I just turn you over to Kenamun now?'

'I have thought of what I would say to you, Ay. I would not have said as much as I have if I did not know that I am not in your power.'

The old man's lip quivered and he turned away again. After a moment he had mastered himself, and now the glittering eyes turned in on themselves again, coldly weighing, as the heart within reached its decision.

'Very well,' he said at last. 'It seems that I must trust you — or give you what passes for trust. You are a very clever man; cleverer than I thought. But you are in a light boat, not on firm land; and there are rapids ahead.'

'Then I must keep a tight grip on my paddle.'

Ay almost smiled. 'Be sure that you do,' he said.

Huy was not allowed to leave until night had fallen. Ineny wanted to escort him home, but it was an easy matter to persuade him not to. As for remaining alone in the palace compound, he still had his badge of office, and he intended to put it to use.

He waited until the shadows were at their deepest before setting out, hugging the walls, for the royal palace.

# SEVEN

Queen Ankhsenpaamun was expecting him. She greeted him in a narrow stone hall, hemmed in by massive painted columns, dwarfing mere humans. She wore a pleated dress of dark blue, with a golden headdress and collar. It was as if she had dressed with such severe formality to bolster her from the shock which, from her expression, she already knew she was going to receive.

She held her hands before her as she approached him, her eyes wide open and shining. He caught her thoughts before she spoke them and there was no need for her to question him. He felt that there was no need for him to tell her, either; but he did, bluntly, briefly. Not adorning the fact or concealing anything. He was past that now.

When he had told her she was still for long minutes, her face taking on an expression of utter desolation; more, thought Huy, than the half-expected news that he had brought would warrant. She looked as if the world had abandoned her.

'There is other news, too,' she said finally, in a voice like the desert.

'What?'

'Prince Zannanzash is dead. His whole party and my couriers were ambushed by desert pirates, and killed and robbed. He had only a light guard with him.'

It was Huy's turn to be silent. Then he said, 'How do you know?'

'His father sent me the news. It is a great sadness.'

'Will there be war?'

'No. But the only reason is that King Shuppiluliumash is not ready. He suspects that the pirates were not there by chance. But he does not blame me.'

'How could he?'

'Indeed. My only thought was for peace, and protection for my child. An alliance with the Hittites would have been the salvation of the Black Land.'

After she had finished speaking she was silent for a while. They stood opposite each other in the bleak stone room, which was cold, and which contained a darkness which even the many oil lamps could not dispel. Her hands went to her stomach, covering it protectively. Her eyes, which had been distant, became hard, and her young face became older.

'What happens now?' she asked, finally.

'You must leave,' said Huy.

'When?' The voice was empty.

'As soon as possible.'

'But not before the entombment?'

'That is at least two months away.'

'I will not leave before the entombment.'

'You must.'

'They have killed the king. You do not understand. They have killed him.' Her eyes were on fire. 'I will not allow them to take his name away, to kill his *Ka* as well.'

'They will not do that.' Huy wanted to tell her that the one thing Tutankhamun was assured of was a proper funeral. That his death had been anything other than an accident would be something only ever known to two or three people, and the secret would die with them. But he could see from her eyes that there would be no point in producing rational arguments for her now. 'The king is safe,' he went on. 'No one can touch his *Ka*. He has gone to join the gods. But you are still here. And you carry the succession within you.'

'Are you telling me that I should flee from these people? I am the queen! I will order their deaths!'

She had flared up now, and Huy was alarmed at the change

87

in her thinking. As gently as he could, aware of the possibility of eavesdropers in the shadows, he tried to make her see the reality of her situation. That she was a prisoner, and that apart from her body servants no one would obey her. She was still too young to accept the facts he placed before her, but by the time he had finished speaking she had grown up a little more.

Her face remained sullen, as if she were reluctant to abandon her thoughts of revenge. Huy hoped that he could persuade her to set them aside for the time being at least. He knew that she would never be in a position to avenge her husband; but there was no reason why she should not remain under the illusion if it helped to ensure her safety. In a distant future it might be that her child could claim its due. After all, it had been two decades before Menkheperre Tuthmosis, greatest of pharaohs, had been able to sit unhindered on the Golden Chair.

The queen accepted his arguments at last, and fuelled with that falsest of elixirs, hope, she agreed to put the safety of her child above the value of her dignity. Huy left her alone in the hall, a tiny mortal surrounded by impossible and vacuous images of grandeur. His only prayer was that the gods would hold her in safety long enough for him to organise her escape; but he did not think that Horemheb or Ay would move against her so soon after the king's death.

Hugging shadows, he made his way back to the harbour quarter and his own house, embracing its isolation and his familiar loneliness like friends as he entered. He drew a woollen rug around his shoulders, for lack of food and sleep had made him cold, and settled his heart by reading. Cocooned by the night, he let his senses drift. At last his eyelids drooped, but a confusion of images jarred him awake again. It was a long time before they let him go.

Huy awoke to find his lamp burnt out and the pale lilac shafts of dawn striking through the window. Stiff from having slept in a chair, he pulled himself to his feet, massaging his neck. His head felt heavy and his intellect was blurred, but after he had bathed and shaved, perfumed himself and put on a clean linen kilt and new palm leaf sandals, he felt better restored than he had done in days.

Senseneb greeted him with surprise, and, he thought, pleasure, though from her face she had slept as little as he had since their last meeting. She looked vulnerable. Perhaps she had been thinking about where her future lay now. It was time that she did. She could not simply have remained her father's daughter, living by his side, forever. The reflection did not make it any easier for Huy to tell her what he had to tell her; nevertheless, it must be done. There was nothing to be gained from keeping the truth from those you wished to enlist as your allies, though that consideration did not give him the courage to speak of her father's murderer straight away.

He reckoned without her perceptiveness. She had called him through her heart once, and now she read his eyes without difficulty.

'You have something important to tell me.'

'Yes.'

'I didn't think you had come simply to find out how I was.' She had turned her face away.

'I would not have needed a greater reason.'

'Nevertheless . . .'

'There is something, yes. And it will hurt.'

'Little could hurt me more than what has already happened.'

'I think I know who killed Horaha.'

'That is not bad news. Tell me.'

'Kenamun.'

'How?'

'He does Horemheb's dirty work. If he was there at the Oblation to Hapy . . .'

'But he would have been there anyway, as a court official. Isn't the connection too obvious?'

'We know Horaha's death was meant as a warning.'

Senseneb looked thoughtful. 'I am sure that my father was

poisoned. There is nothing I can prove. If Kenamun — or someone used by him — could have poisoned the sacred river water he drank . . .'

'I would like to finish Kenamun,' said Huy. 'For this, and for other crimes.'

'Let me help you,' she said. 'You tell me that you think he killed my father, and I believe you. Horaha has no one but me to avenge him.'

'It will be hard to bring Kenamun down.'

They were sitting in the garden, in the same place as he had first met her with her father. Now she stood up, and paced the length of the pool impatiently. Returning to him, she said, 'There is Ay.'

'Yes.'

'Have you seen him?'

'Yes.'

'What deal have you made with him?'

She had sat down again now, still impatient, her whole body taut, her long legs spread like a man's, leaning forward, forearms on thighs, her head low, at an angle, looking up at him, her eyes dark and angry.

'I have asked for more time.'

'Why?'

Huy spread his hands. He was telling her more than he had wanted to, but found that he could not help it. It was possible too that he was tired of having no one in whom he could place trust. There was Nehesy, but he was part of the palace. Senseneb had suffered at the hands of the authorities and she was now outside them. The law, society, would no longer protect her, for she had seen it for what it was in its present guise; and she, too, needed someone to trust. Suffering is intolerable when it is endured in isolation, thought Huy; and action to end it needs help.

'I asked for more time because I want to get Ay's measure. He has a hold over me which I do not like. If for any reason Horemheb gets wind of what I know, or of what I am doing, before Ay is ready, Ay will toss me to him without a thought. By placating Horemheb he could buy *himself* more time.'

'But don't you have enough on Horemheb to give Ay now? Enough for him to use to bring the general down?'

'I think so. But my knowledge is also my safe conduct. I know that Ay is hungry to be king. I must let that hunger grow greater before I feed it. Then, instead of my being in his power, he will be in mine.'

To his surprise, he found that Senseneb was looking at him with contempt. 'I see,' she said, tonelessly.

'What do you see?'

She rounded on him. 'You are playing the game like an expert, Huy. The only thing I do not understand is why you are so candid with me.'

'What do you mean?' Huy had been too intent on explaining his plan. He now found that he had explained it appallingly.

'What will your price to Horemheb be? Kenamun's head?'

'For what?'

She laughed. 'For Ay! I will not avenge my father through another betrayal.'

Huy was too tired to restrain himself. Fury seized him. He stood up, grabbed the woman by the shoulders and shook her hard. She broke loose and hit him with a balled fist across the mouth. He responded immediately, not thinking, feeling his right arm swing and the impact of his open hand on the side of her head. He felt briefly the softness of her cheek and the texture of her hair. He had caught her squarely off balance and she sprawled on to the couch. Before she could recover he took her roughly by the arm above the elbow and pulled her up, jerking her savagely round to face him.

'What are you thinking? Has grief deranged you? If I cannot convince you I am not evil at least understand that I am not stupid. Do you seriously believe that I could play one regent off against the other like that? They would close ranks and crush me and then continue their battle with each other. As for Kenamun, I pray the good gods to let me find a way to get him; but not as a price to Horemheb for Ay!'

She glared at him silently, her mouth defiant; but gradually thought replaced anger in her eyes, and both their bodies relaxed. When he released her, he was shocked to see the ugly purple marks his fingers had made on her arm.

'I thought you could read my heart,' he said.

'So did I. I could not believe what I saw there.'

'You saw what you put there. What we are involved in now is cobra's venom; it seeps into us too.'

'You are not above using it.'

'To survive, yes. For my own advancement, no. Not because I am moral. Because I am practical. That kind of advancement carries its own chains, its own death.'

Senseneb drew herself upright on the couch, curling her legs round her. Her body was smooth muscled, like a panther's. The plain white mourning robe she wore had pulled tightly against her in their struggle, and she made no attempt to loosen it again. Perhaps she was not even aware of it.

'The queen,' Huy began, 'the queen must leave here before she is killed. I do not think she is in danger until after the pharaoh's funeral but I am not going to take the chance. To Horemheb she is a threat until he can father a new child. In any case he will want to get rid of her because a son or daughter in direct line from Tutankhamun could always gather forces against him. And for the same reason Ay would not flinch from killing her, if marriage to her proves impossible. But he is her grandfather, and there is a shred of hope that he could be manoeuvred into showing mercy.'

'How?'

'If he were convinced that she would not be a threat. He is more subtle than Horemheb and less ruthless. He is an artist, not a scientist. He is less predictable, weaker, more malleable. Above all he is vain. And as long as the general and the Master of Horse are preoccupied with each other, there is a chance that the queen may slip out between them. That is why I am playing for time.'

Her eyes were as dark as sloes. 'I do not know why you trust me. You are too clever to trust anyone. Why are you telling me this?'

Huy was too weary of explanation to explain any more. He could not tell her that his ideas were only half thought out, that at any minute they might founder, that they were based on supposition and the hope of fortunate coincidences, that after all he was an inexperienced opportunist in too deep and principally motivated by a desire to survive. It was true that in the midst of all that were a desire to see the queen safe, and a desire to kill Kenamun, but nothing was in focus.

'I am telling you because you of all people could not use it against me. Your father was disinterested, showed integrity, and died for it. Who on earth is going to trust you after that?'

'You spawn of Set,' said Senseneb after studying his face in silence for a moment or two.

Huy laughed. 'Now you don't believe me.'

'But what you say is so possible.'

'Yes; but is the reasoning?'

'Coming from you?' She smiled. 'I honestly don't know any more.'

Huy had sat down in the chair near the couch. Now he leant forward to pour the wine which Hapu had placed there when he arrived.

'Isn't it a little early for that?' asked Senseneb, putting her feet on the ground and sitting up.

'Yesterday was very long,' said Huy. He sipped the drink he had poured and leant back, looking at the girl. Two or three strands of hair had swept across her face and she shook her head to clear them. He gazed at the columns of her neck and the collarbones that spanned her wide shoulders, then he became aware of her gaze and looked away, uncomfortably. He had become relaxed at last and here, in this delightful garden which Senseneb would only be able to enjoy for a short time more, he felt that the walls were enough to shut out the rest of the world – at least for that morning. His eyes were drawn back to her. The expression on her face was veiled, but her heart was speaking to him again and its message was clear. He put down his cup, rose, and crossed to sit next to her, touching her arm where a bruise was already developing. Her eyes were lowered, her breath was warm. She moved her head gently forwards and touched his nose with hers. Then she kissed him, fully, open-mouthed, but still lightly and quickly, drawing away as soon as she had done so. His nostrils were filled with the smell of her, close and delicious.

'Not here,' she said, standing and drawing him up with her. 'My room is more comfortable.'

They hurried to the house, stomachs hollow with excitement, both needing to bury the tension and sadness of the last few days in love. The house was empty and Huy wondered what had happened to the servants – could they all have left already, except Hapu? Again she caught his thought as they reached her door on the verandah, and smiled. 'I wanted you, and so as soon as you arrived I told Hapu to send everyone away for the morning. I know I may sound a little crazy but when I make love I like to be alone with my lover.'

The catch of the door would not give at first and she rattled it in a fit of impatience. Inside, the room was cool and white; the bed was covered with fresh sheets of soft linen. Once the door was shut, Seneseneb became the panther under her skin. The mourning robe was shrugged off in one movement. In one more she had slipped her arms round him and with cunning, hungry, practised hands taken his kilt away and embraced the Worshipper of Min between his thighs. Her lips were on his neck, plunging and sucking, and he fell back as she straddled him. All that she did had a lithe, violent impatience. She slid down his body, never removing her lips and tongue from his skin, until her mouth found him, taking him deep within her, cushioning him on her tongue, caressing his balls with one cool firm hand, while the other encircled the root of his manhood.

94

His heart reeled, partly because of the distance from reality which exhaustion brings, partly from her demands on him, to which he was responding, to his astonishment and delight, with as much enthusiasm as they were made.

'I want you.'
'I want you.'
'I love you.'
'I love you.'
'Give me yourself.'
'Give me yourself.'

He curved his body and found the entrance of her birth-cave with his tongue. Her tongue fondled the tip of his penis while he caressed her clitoris with his. Satisfied at last with the joining of the upper and lower openings, they turned to face each other, and Renenutet joined them where a man and a woman have their core.

For one hour they buried themselves in each other, and when they finally ceased, they looked into each others' eyes like happy, wary animals, finding trust there, but also danger and mystery. She turned from him, presenting strong buttocks, and supporting herself on her arms turned her head over one shoulder to issue her next command. Past thinking, he seized her flanks and then her breasts so hard that she gasped, and gave himself to her again, feeling her softness against his hard stomach, while she reached below them to stroke him.

Still when he withdrew, neither had finished with the other, though the appetite as another hour passed became less voracious, more refined. They became aware of details: beads of sweat on a shoulder to lick off; pungent droplets in the tousle of hair between her legs and his. Their hands clasped each other like mouths which could not be satisfied; they kissed until their tongues' roots ached. Each part of their bodies, each smooth curve, glistening, lubricated, became an empire of delight.

At last they were raw, bruised, battered, sore, sleepy, laughing, content, and lay still. He drew a sheet over them as the sweat cooled on their bodies, and they curled up together in the arms of night.

Neither had been aware for one moment of the figure watching them from beyond the window.

At the same time one of the Black Medjays kicked Nehesy hard in the stomach. His left eye was already split and closed, and they had sliced off one ear with a knife. Blood filled his mouth and he could hardly see. His heart was filled with a dark cloud, through which pain drove in the form of brilliant light. It had been worst when they pushed the needles under his fingernails.

'You are in an ugly mess but at least you are still alive. We could patch you up, let you go, even give you your job back.' Kenamun's voice was patient, but it an edge now. It was three hours since they had brought Nehesy here and still, in this back room of Horemheb's palace, its dun walls smeared with more blood than Kenamun would have thought possible if they had slaughtered an ox, the big man had refused to talk.

Strapped on his back to a heavy wooden table, Nehesy heard the voice, but it came from beyond the stars. His tongue, which he had bitten hard in his attempt to conquer his pain, and then again by accident, had swollen to fill his mouth. It no longer belonged to him; it was a lolling thing, large and clumsy, a beast in pain that had lodged inside him. His stomach, bruised and smashed, felt as if it contained folded paper. Far away below him and to his sides, his arms and legs sent back dull signals of distress. He managed to mumble something. His torn ear thundered with pain.

'He's finished,' said the sergeant in charge of the detail, nervously. Kenamun took a serrated knife and sawed off Nehesy's left hand. The huntsman bellowed with agony.

'No, he isn't,' said Kenamun. 'Plenty of life left there.' He brought his face close to Nehesy's, smelling his sweat and blood with excitement and distaste, thinking how much more he would enjoy doing this to a woman. But he was frightened too.

Someone had found out too much. Getting rid of the doctor had not been enough.

Kenamun drew back and glanced round the drab room, wiping his knife clean on a rag. He caught a look of fear and contempt on the sergeant's face, and noted that here was another not to be trusted. How quickly the numbers of them spiralled; those who were fine at the start but who turned out not to have the stomach for seeing the thing through. Perhaps in the end the only ones they would be able to depend on would be found within the ranks of the distant Delta army. But the two other torturers were younger – brawny, square-shouldered, ox-headed men from Busiris. They had shown no qualms during the session. They had beaten Nehesy so hard with their truncheons at the outset that it had even been necessary to restrain them. Now, they were wrapping linen rags round their fists to protect their palms from the wire lashes they were preparing to use.

Nehesy was huge. His bulk was increased by the swellings from the beating he had been given. Thinking of women, Kenamun felt again the disgust and excitement which tightened every muscle in his body.

'Not the wire,' said Kenamun.

He showed them what to do himself. Putting a foot in Nehesy's right armpit, he pulled slowly at the man's wrist until the arm was out of joint at the shoulder. 'If you can yell, you can talk,' he spat at Nehesy; but the big man had passed out.

The assistants threw water over him.

'Now do the same to his right leg,' said Kenamun. The sergeant left the room abruptly. Kenamun's expression did not change. He watched them twist Nehesy's leg until it hung limp.

'Will you tell us who knows?'

Nehesy did not reply, but his eye still glittered. Kenamun watched as he opened his mouth to speak, but knew that nothing would come out – not because the huntsman could not talk; but because he was still not broken.

Kenamun sighed, and took a small gadget from the table he stood at: two flat pieces of wood joined by thin wire, and a stick. He wrapped the wire under Nehesy's left knee and twisted it tight with the stick until blood and muscle burst out and the wire grated on bone. Nehesy screamed with a violence and at a volume which made even the hard skulls of the young torturers crawl.

'Save yourself,' Kenamun said softly, after the scream had subsided into a sobbing whimper. 'Bravery never mattered, never changed anything. Why give yourself all this grief?'

Nehesy spoke at last, bringing his torturer into focus. 'May Set shit in your mouth.'

Kenamun blinked once. Perhaps the man really knew nothing. But no, that could not be. He was an experienced huntsman, he had been with the king on the last expedition. He was bound to have had suspicions. Inwardly, the police chief cursed. They had been too confident, too arrogant.

'He can't take any more now,' he said. 'Give him an hour.' He looked at Nehesy. 'Show some sense then, or we'll start on your teeth. Then your other eye. Then your prick. Think about it.'

'Shall we clean him up?' asked one of the thugs as he turned to go. Was he imagining more faintheartedness?

'No,' said Kenamun.

# EIGHT

'Why?' Ineny drank fastidiously from his cup of pomegranate wine. 'Because I don't think he will have the courage to do anything in the end. That is why.'

Huy, sitting across from him, looked out to where the River had turned a deeper shade of red. The flood was coming. Soon it would be upon them. The chroniclers and measurers of the inundation predicted a strong rise in the water level this year. There would be a good crop later. Peasants talked of the departed pharaoh's last gift to his people. But in the city the talk was of his successor. Too much time had passed without a nomination, though that morning the official inquiry into Tutankhamun's death had at last come up with its unsurprising finding: death by misadventure.

'People are becoming impatient,' continued Ineny. 'If Ay does not move soon he will lose initiative and perhaps the chance to move at all.'

'It is better to prepare your ground before you move, to be certain that your footing will be sure.'

'Oh, of course,' said Ineny sarcastically. Huy returned his smile. They had met by chance in the street that afternoon, and Ineny had invited him to share a bottle. It had been an excuse for two off-duty employees to swap opinions about their master. Ineny had thrown off all reserve, and now, relaxed, chatting, he was a different person. At first it had been Huy who had held up his guard, since a chance meeting of this type very often turned out to be arranged; but if it had been Ineny's intention to pump him, then either he was very bad at it or he had been sidetracked by his own preoccupations, because nothing had been demanded of Huy other than polite interjections and the occasional bland statement, to show that he was paying attention.

Ineny was principally affected by the consideration that he had thrown in his lot with the wrong man. Huy sought to reassure him and retain his trust without appearing to be too anxious to do so. Ineny was in on too many of Huy's secrets to be treated off-handedly.

'I always wondered if he'd have the courage to stand up to Horemheb,' he was saying mournfully. 'Now I'm proved right. But it's too late for me to change sides. I'm a marked man.'

'Do you really want to?'

'I want to get on. That means following the right leader.'

'I wouldn't give up Ay yet.'

Ineny looked at him, and drank some more wine. 'I've been with him since he returned to the Southern Capital. He was always so hungry for power – he managed his life so well. But now that the Golden Chair is within his grasp, he hesitates.'

'Gathering strength before he jumps.'

'Do you think so?' Ineny raised his eyebrows hopefully just as Huy was beginning to think that he had thrown in one platitude too many. But for Huy there was nothing disappointing in Ay's caution. It was to his caution that Huy owed his survival. However, he was not going to spell that out for Ineny. He would be interested to see which way the little man would jump. Ineny was a small piece on the *senet* board; but he was in an important position.

Huy could not afford to relax. He knew the real reason for Ay's hesitation – Ineny had not been present for all of his own interview with the old Master of Horse – and he also knew that Ay's patience would run out as soon as he sensed the moment to strike was passing. Huy would have to give Ay all the information he had within the next two days. To do that and guarantee the safety of the queen would require quick thinking.

'Has Ay asked after me since our last meeting?'

'No. But don't think for a moment that he has forgotten you.' Ineny smiled. 'I admire you, Huy. All this time we have been talking I find that I've opened my soul to you – such as it is. And you manage to be a pleasant companion, cordial, even warm – and yet at the end of it I know not one grain more about you than I did to begin with.'

'You would make a poor spy, Ineny.'

'My wits have not disappointed me so far.'

'Stay with Ay. It would be foolish to make more enemies than you need to at a time like this.'

'I do not ask your advice.'

'Then why have you told me all this?'

'What is it you know, Huy?'

'Very little.' Huy managed to remain close-faced. But Ineny's restlessness worried him. To take the man into his confidence demanded too great a risk for him to take now. If it turned out later that he regretted his caution, he would accept what the gods arranged. In the meantime Huy would need all the help he could get from the one person he had decided he could trust without any reserve: Nehesy. Senseneb too, perhaps; but she knew enough about medicine to procure and administer poison, and she would not be the first woman to use sex to turn a potential enemy's judgement. Huy had not forgotten Merinakhte, the young doctor who had climbed as high as he could and whose eye would now be on his next goal – Horaha's position. Had he enlisted Senseneb's help to get it?

He shook himself like a dog to cleanse his heart. It was surely not good, not healthy, to see the dark side of everything Ra sent.

For Ay, it was a difficult interview. He had rehearsed it in his heart many times before facing it in reality, and now had to acknowledge that reality has the disadvantage of having no script.

The step he was attempting to take was one which he had

101

considered at length, and he had discussed it with his Chief Wife. Tey had acquiesced, but with reserve, and Ay was left with the feeling that although she had always supported him in his ambitions, she drew the line at agreeing to give up her primacy as a stepping stone. Still, the speed with which Ankhsenpaamun had put her plan to marry the Hittite prince into action had alarmed him. If Ineny had not got wind of it through the royal body servant he slept with, Prince Zannanzash might be in the Southern Capital even now, sending messages about his safe arrival back to his ever more powerful father. An accidental death here would have been out of the question, and it would not have been long before not only he, but Horemheb, would have felt the earth open beneath them.

For a while he had hesitated, hardly daring to believe that Horemheb's spies had not got wind of the queen's plot too — and then when he was sure, he had hesitated again; but finally he had given the order to have Zannanzash killed, because Horemheb's downfall would not necessarily have ensured his own survival; and with Zannanzash enthroned, Ay's own hope of the Golden Chair would vanish forever.

But the incident had shown him how essential it was for him to strengthen his links with the royal family. It was his own lowly birth which had failed to secure him the succession when Akhenaten had died. He would not make the mistake of overlooking that again. He did not have the time! Age hung like a clinging ape around his shoulders, weighing him down, and no amount of make-up, exercise or a frugal diet could keep the lines from the neck, the forehead and the elbows, or could prevent the skin from sagging at the jowls and losing its elasticity on the hands, or stop the biceps from turning into loose, flabby folds. Ay had his hair dyed, and under his robe he wore a tight linen bandage to hold in his shocking balloon of a stomach, which would not decrease even though he only ate one small meal of rice and figs a day, and drank nothing but water.

\*     \*     \*

Ankhsenpaamun received Ay formally, with a retinue of body servants. That disquieted him. He had little doubt that she knew why he had come, and was irritated at her insistence on addressing him as 'grandfather'. After the formal greetings were out of the way, he managed to persuade her to dismiss most of the people, though she kept two women near, one of whom kept darting impertinent glances at him from a plain face whose bright black eyes reminded him of a rodent's. Ay, wishing that he had at least one supporter with him, toyed with the beaker of Kharga wine he had been offered and been obliged to accept, wondering if he could get away without drinking it. He looked into the queen's unfriendly eyes and wondered if she had guessed the truth about what had happened to Zannanzash. He decided that even if she suspected a killing, it was more likely that she would blame Horemheb than him.

'I do not see why you wish to take a new wife,' said Ankhsenpaamun, once he had made his proposal.

'The answer to that is simple,' replied Ay. 'Your safety. By marrying me, you would be sure of my protection.'

'And after your death, grandfather? We are separated by fifty years.'

Despite the coldness of his desire, for Ay had hardly considered this marriage as one which would involve the two of them sharing the love bond, her words caught at his heart. How merciless youth is, how arrogant is its energy, he thought. And yet looking at his granddaughter he remembered Nefertiti, and her mother, who had died so very young, an age ago, when he had himself been young, or at least clinging to the shreds of youth, at thirty-five.

'I will not die so soon.'

'And what about my child?'

'It will be safe.'

'And the succession?'

Now she had touched a nerve. Ay had no son. It was true that he had seen his other daughter marry his rival, so that perhaps one way or another his blood would flow in future generations on the Golden Chair; but Nezemmut's child had died as it entered this world. That was a bad omen, and although the girl was young, and broad-hipped, the old man still clung to a hope of siring his own successors. His Chief Wife, Tey, was too old for more children; but could he manage to bring his granddaughter to bed? His principal intention in marrying her was to strengthen his own bond with the Golden Chair, but . . .

Ay gnawed at the idea, then put it back. First things first. Let him marry this girl and sit on the throne. A strategy to secure it for his direct descendants could be developed later; and anyway Horemheb would be a danger while he was alive. Fleetingly, he thought of Huy. How much depended now on that little spy's evidence.

'The succession lies in your birth-cave,' he said. He had barely hesitated a second before replying.

The queen pursed her lips. 'That would be a condition of our marriage.'

'I loved the king like a son.'

'That I have never doubted,' she replied, with equal formality, though her voice was taut.

'Then you will accept me?'

'I need time to consider it.'

'There isn't time. Tutankhamun's successor must be named.'

'Why can there not be a regency again until my child is old enough to rule?'

There is not time, thought Ay. He wanted to seize her by the shoulders, shake her, chase all that youthful insouciance out of her. How dare she be so unruffled by the passing of time? He felt the touch of Osiris on his shoulder every hour now. Well, one day this cocky little girl would do so too.

'It would be unwise. The country needs to feel unified behind a pharaoh again. One strong enough to face the threat from the north.'

'I see. And you are that man?'

'It would be best, if our family is to keep the crown.'

'And what about my aunt?'

'Nezemmut is – '

'What? An understudy? A second string to your bow?'

'The king your husband willed that she should marry Horemheb, not I.'

Ankhsenpaamun turned away. She felt disgusted and trapped. Mistaking her movement for modesty, coyness, girlish indecision, Ay stretched out what he hoped was a fatherly hand. She felt it on her bare shoulder, dry, warm and leathery, like a snake sliding there. She shrank from it. Understanding immediately, humiliated and furious, but as much for the damage done to his scheme as for himself, Ay withdrew.

'Consider my offer,' he said stiffly, after a pause, lowering his voice so the two women attendants (who stood stiff as statues three or four paces away, but whose eyes, he knew, had missed nothing) could not hear. 'Accept it is your best hope of safety, and the best security for the Black Land.'

The queen trembled, though whether with rage or fear Ay could not tell. 'I cannot,' she said finally, and her voice, though firm, was toneless.

'You do not have a choice,' retorted Ay, harshly. 'I will give you five days to reconsider. If you refuse me you risk much.'

Feeling that with this threat he had gone too far, he brought their conversation to an abrupt end, with only as much ceremony as was necessary to prevent the observers' tongues wagging, and left her. Pointedly, he did not bother to reach the door before turning his back.

Ankhsenpaamun managed to hold back her tears long enough to dismiss the women, then she let go and threw herself on to a chair, giving way to the anger, grief, frustration and loneliness which she could bear no longer.

'Nehesy isn't here any more,' said the stable boy with the carbuncle to Huy. They stood in the dusty yard. Over it all there hung an air of neglect, disuse. Huy looked across to the animal shed, and wondered how the beasts there were faring.

'Where has he gone?'

The man scratched his neck. Huy noticed that two among the cluster of boils had started to fester. The man needed medical treatment quickly, or he would risk gangrene. 'They took him away.'

'Who did?'

'I thought you were a palace official. The Medjays did.'

'Arrested him?'

'Yes.'

'When?'

Scratching again, and squinting into the sun, the man said, 'Four days ago.'

'Did you find out what for?'

'Do they need a reason nowadays?'

Huy glanced towards the huntsman's house.

'No good looking there,' said the stable boy. 'The family's gone too.'

'What?'

'Yes. There's a new chief huntsman.'

'Who?'

The man grinned. 'Me. Don't look so alarmed. No one's got time for hunting just now so I'm a sort of caretaker. This thing on my neck's going to put me into the Boat of the Night before I'm much older, anyway.'

'You could have it treated.'

'I haven't time to leave the animals. Somebody's got to keep them clean and fed and exercised.'

'But what'll happen afterwards?'

The man shrugged. 'Everyone's got to die sooner or later. I expect they'll appoint somebody, once they've settled whose going to rule us. There'll always be hunting, whoever's in charge.'

'What's happened to Nehesy's wife? Where's she gone?'

'Her parents have a farm just north of the city.'

106

'I don't even know her name.'

'Aahetep, if it's any use to you. But she's got no more idea why they took Nehesy than I have.'

Huy hurried back through the city. The sun at midday was so harsh by this time in the season that all activity ceased until the breeze picked up again towards evening. Business was compressed into the hours of the early *matet* boat and the late *seqtet* boat. It was now late in the morning so the streets were clearing, and although the rickshaw puller he had hired grumbled unceasingly under his breath at the mercilessness of expecting him to drive in this heat, they covered the distance between the palace and the northern streets of the town in fewer than thirty minutes.

The city ended abruptly. The sheer walls of the houses, elevated on their low hill of centuries of detritus and the rubble of earlier buildings, which protected them from the worst of the annual river floods, gave way immediately to fields which were parched and cracked now, but which would very soon be flooded with the rich black silt which was the life-giving gift of Hapy. The River had risen already, the red sand which gave it its colour at this time of year swirling on its surface as it passed northward on its long journey to the Great Green.

As Huy walked along its shore he startled a flock of egrets which rose white in the sun on silent wings, only mildly irritated by the disturbance, to settle again a handful of paces further on. From this new position they paid no more attention to him.

On the distant west bank it was just possible to make out the dun forms of herons, but only when one of them abandoned its still-as-stone posture to dart at a fish, or rose in unhurried flight to curl above the implacable rocks of the valley beyond. Near the shores, duck and geese swam, scooping the surface of the River for food, and farther downstream, where smooth rocks shelved to the water's edge, crocodiles basked in the sun, warming themselves for the evening's hunt. Near them, coots scuttled through the current in nervous teams.

A handful of villages, thatched mud buildings the colour of

the land, clutched the ground in tight clusters on either bank, and there was a number of isolated farms which lay closer to the protection of the town. Wrapping his scarf around his head to protect himself from the heat, Huy kicked the dust out of his sandals and set off for the nearest one.

The furious barking of dogs which heralded his approach worried him, but the animals – two large black brutes of a kind he did not recognise – were tied to a hefty stake in the middle of the farmyard. There was no one about, which was not surprising in view of the time of day, so Huy, skirting the buildings – a simple low house flanked by a barn – in order to keep out of the dogs' range, made his way to the nearest door and knocked. The dogs, aware that further action was impossible, retired to their patch of shade after loping around for a minute, and from there glared at him threateningly before giving up the whole idea, and lowering their heads on to their paws.

The farmer was a brittle stick of a man, the colour of sweet wood and fuddled with sleep. He had been up since four, preparing his land for the coming flood, after which the country would swelter, sweating and harassed by mosquitoes, until Hapy passed on his way and the season of growth could begin. Huy had noticed the complicated system of irrigation ditches and slender canals which linked them, now dry and neglected, as he had left the city, and imagined the activity that would animate this countryside five months later, when the waters would have withdrawn, and planting could begin, following a frenzied cleaning and redigging of the veins and arteries of the country's body.

Aahetep's parents' farm lay further out from the city, but Huy was just able to discern it through the heat haze by squinting in the direction the farmer pointed.

'But you can't go now. Look where the sun is,' said the farmer; and indeed the heat had suspended all life. The birds had disappeared from the shore, the crocodiles had withdrawn into deep shade or slunk into the water, where the tiny blisters

108

made on the surface by their eyes were all that betrayed their presence. The farm dogs had become metamorphosed into low dark rocks.

Huy shook his head. 'I must.'

'The heat will be too much.'

'There is no time to wait. And I think they will not be sleeping.'

'The parents perhaps. Raia and Tutu have as much to do as we have; but the daughter . . .' he broke off. 'There has been a tragedy.'

'What sort of tragedy?' asked Huy.

The farmer regarded him coolly. 'I thought you city folk knew everything. A death in the family. She's got their little boy with her.'

'Can I hire your donkey?'

The walnut face looked at him, and the farmer spat. 'Not in this heat, you can't. But have some water before you set out.'

Huy walked slowly, forcing himself not to hurry, knowing that the faster he went, the less chance he stood of making it, though the two farmsteads were not more than a thousand paces apart. He had spread his shawl to cover his back and neck as well as his head, and he had wet it in one of the farmer's water jars, so that the going was not too bad, though the heat of the soil scorched his feet through his sandals. Long before he reached the other farm his shawl was dry and his lips and mouth were losing their moisture. Squinting against the sun as he approached the other farmhouse, Huy saw a pair of vultures wheeling high and far away to the north east. Specks that vanished and reappeared as they flew in and out of the sunlight. What dying thing out there had caught their attention?

Raia's dogs raised their heads at his approach and managed an exhausted growl, but allowed him to approach the house door without any other challenge. This farm was larger than the first, and small numbers of livestock were corralled in pens under palm leaf umbrellas about the yard. A slim white pig lay in the corner of one, fast asleep, its ears over its eyes. In another, five geese started up, staring at him with beady, intelligent eyes. It was a long time before anyone answered his knock, but at last the door opened a crack to reveal a pale face framed in ragged, undressed hair. The woman held a small child of about three on one arm.

'Aahetep?'

'Who are you?'

'Huy. A friend of Nehesy.'

Her eyes flickered into life and pain at the mention of her husband's name, but she must have picked something up from Huy's tone for no suspicion or enmity appeared in them, and she stood back, opening the door a fraction wider. Closing it behind him, the child staring at him inquisitively, she led the way through an inner courtyard hung about with farm implements to a long low room facing north on the other side of the house. From a gallery half in shadow came the noise of snoring from one end and the rustle of straw as a body resting on it shifted its position in sleep.

'My parents are there.'

'I know.'

The child burbled. Fearful that he might speak, or cry out, the girl took him to a small bed set against the wall, where he settled down, though from it he continued to gaze at Huy with the bright, frank eyes of his father. Then she returned to sit opposite her visitor, her own eyes tired, and their expression dull.

'I am Nehesy's friend,' said Huy again.

She shifted her position. 'He spoke of you.'

'Is he in trouble?'

'What have you come for?'

'To find out what has happened to him.'

An expression of great bitterness crossed her face, which Huy did not understand. 'If you do not know, you are either a *very* good friend, or no friend at all.'

'We were working together. I went to the stables and

110

they told me he had been arrested. So I came here to find out more.'

She continued to look at him bleakly, as if gathering the energy to speak. When she finally did, it was in a low, toneless voice, wrung dry of feeling.

'Four days ago they came to our house at dawn. Three Medjays. They took my husband away. Then at noon one of the officers returned and told me that Nehesy was being relieved of his duties. I would have to get out of the house by evening. I didn't know where to go. When something like that happens with things as they are at the moment, none of your friends wants to know you. So I came home here. They knew where I'd gone at the stables so I supposed that sooner or later Nehesy would be released, and would join me – I knew he couldn't have done any harm – or that I'd be given news. I waited a day and then I went to the city, but no one could tell me anything.'

All the time she spoke in a voice of quiet bewilderment, as if she could not believe that such a thing could have happened to her secure little family.

'And then,' she continued after a pause in which she had taken several deep breaths, 'yesterday they brought him home.' She stopped speaking again, and looked with dead eyes at a point in the room behind Huy.

'Where is he now?'

'In the stable. Below the loft.'

'How is he? Is he sleeping?'

Her eyes met his again. 'Yes. He is sleeping.'

Suddenly a cold fear gripped Huy's heart. 'What did they do to him?'

'They told me he fell from a gallery in the prison. He was being escorted to an interview with one of the investigators and he slipped and fell.'

'Did they tell you what he was accused of?'

Aahetep hung her head. 'I was afraid to ask. They never look into your eyes. They look at your forehead and talk to you as if

111

your existence was something which they can't bring themselves to acknowledge. They told me that as a servant of the state, he was entitled to a funeral at the expense of the palace. I told them I preferred to keep him.'

'What will you do?'

She looked at him with tired pride. 'We cannot all lie in stone vaults for eternity. This evening my father will dig a pit in the fields, above the floodline. We will line it with stone and my mother and I will weave a wicker roof for it, which we will seal with pitch and cover with sand. Under it Nehesy will lie, curled as he was in his mother, with food and utensils for the great journey. We have no need of embalmers, for the sand will dry him. Geb will take him in his arms and from above Nut will watch over him. Little Itet and I will always be near him, and this house will harbour his *Ka*. It is better than a tomb, and less lonely.'

Huy looked at her. 'Can I see him?'

Without another word she rose, and after a glance at the child, now sleeping, led the way out of the room and across the yard. As she pushed open the stable door, the smell met them and Huy felt his throat tighten. An image came to him before he could repress it of the grey worms seething in eye sockets, but as he approached his friend's body he saw that Nehesy had been spared that.

He lay on his side in an oval wicker basket, his hands cupped under his head and his knees drawn up to his chest. They had sprinkled natron over him, and the big earthenware water jars which stood about him like sentinels kept the temperature in the stable cool. The light was dim, but there was enough for Huy to see what had been done to Nehesy before he died. He stole a glance at Aahetep, looking down at the corpse with moist eyes which still would not acknowledge the truth of what they saw, and wondered if she really believed what they had told her.

'It must have been a very bad fall,' he said.

She looked at him with eyes blazing. 'If you were his friend, may Horus help you avenge him,' she said; and he knew that

112

there was nothing at all he could tell her, even if he had wanted to.

Huy spent that evening at his house with Senseneb. The dinner he had planned had been arranged much earlier, but their anticipation of it had dwindled. They sat near one another after they had eaten, but they spoke little, so preoccupied with their own thoughts that they were not curious about each other's. Huy, glad that after so long there was a woman here again, and one who warmed the little rooms by her presence, still weighed on the scales of his heart the element of risk he would take in confiding in her completely. It seemed to him that he would have to commit himself. There was no progress without risk; his one sure ally had been removed from the field; and Senseneb had done nothing – apparently – to betray him, or they would not have taken Nehesy and tortured him to death.

There was something more: within him he felt the love bond with a woman more strongly than he had since the first years of his long-dead marriage. He still tried to suppress it. There was no time for love now, or so he told himself. But another part of his heart longed for Horaha's daughter, and it would not be quiet.

Senseneb was aware of the distance the present silence had put between them, but she was trying to summon up the courage to share the thoughts which were preoccupying her. She had drunk enough of the Kharga wine he had served to feel confident, but not enough to feel reckless. She did not know what his reaction would be to the truth about her own past. But she reflected that she knew little of his, and was therefore not inhibited in her feelings for him. He did not seem to be a narrow-hearted man, and in any case she would have to gamble to stand any chance of winning.

Both knew that if they parted, or moved on to lovemaking, before they had spoken to each other, an important moment would have been missed forever; but it was difficult to arrive at it. It seemed, they both thought, foolish for two adults who

113

no longer had the excuse of youthful inexperience still to be so much at the mercy of the mischief of Hathor. But they continued to fence, each refusing to begin, discontentedly throwing scraps of small talk into the silence.

The lamp began to flicker and die on the table. Huy dressed the wick, refilling the bowl with linseed oil. The dying light was a reminder of passing time, and the activity it demanded triggered the conversation which had been waiting with increasing impatience to begin.

'More wine?' asked Huy.

'Yes.'

He fetched a fresh jar and broached it, and they drank in continued silence for a moment longer; but both were tired of it now.

'I want to tell you about my past,' said Senseneb. 'I do not need to hear yours in return, though I would like to.'

'I will tell you everything. There is nothing particularly evil, daring or adventurous in it, though. It has been part battle, part assault course, like everyone else's.'

Senseneb smiled. 'I like your house.'

'You honour it.'

She sighed, already thinking that it would be good to live with him; but unsure if there would ever be a time when they could.

'If we are to know each other properly, you must also know my past,' she insisted. 'My parents are now both dead; but there is nothing I have to say to harm their reputations here or in the Fields of Aarru.' As she spoke she looked into the shadows of the room, as if seeking Horaha's *Ba* there, perched on a shelf or clinging bat-like to the wall near the ceiling, listening to his orphan daughter. She knew that he had liked Huy.

'I am twenty-eight,' she said, looking at the lamp. 'My husband sent me back to my parents because I was barren. But that was not the real reason. I had slept with another man; I had slept with several others.'

She looked at Huy's face; but if it was wearing any

expression at all that she could read, it was one of kind-ness.

'I am not barren. We never made love. We slept first with our backs turned to one another, then in separate beds, and at last in separate rooms. But I had a need. And it was not a marriage.'

'When did it end?'

'Two years ago. But it lasted seven.'

'That is long.'

She smiled. 'I have become a middle-aged woman.'

'No.'

'Do you have children?'

'I have a boy. Heby. But it is long since I have seen him.'

They were silent once more, but it was a different kind of silence now.

'Have you thought about what you will do?' asked Huy.

It might depend on you, said her heart, but her voice replied, 'No. There is the house in Napata, in the south, which my father has left me. Perhaps I will go there. I have had enough of this city.'

Huy nodded. Outside the window the waning moon filled the street with grey light. Some small animal, probably a dog, clicked by, its paws tapping out a regular rhythm on the hard ground. Nothing else stirred.

'What will you do in Napata?'

Senseneb smiled. 'I may be a doctor there. I am not leaving all my father's drugs and instruments and papers for his successor.' Her voice became hard, and her eyes turned inwards.

'Why? Who is he?'

'Merinakhte.'

Huy paused before speaking again, trying to read her face. She let him do it, pretending to study the little statue of Bes which stood guard on a shelf. 'Will you help me?'

She turned her eyes to his. 'How?'

'I must get the queen away from here.'

She reached out her hands to him and he took them.

115

'Yes, I will help you. I will live and die for you.'

'And I for you.'

A ferry had crossed between them. They talked more; he told her about Nehesy, about Ay. He told her almost all that he had discovered, but at the back of his heart he knew that from now on they would have to be careful. He could not allow himself to imagine what would happen if Kenamun found out that she knew him. Huy told her about his life, and the City of the Horizon, and how above all he wanted to be a scribe again, and about Heby, and how he still missed him, even though he had no idea what his son must look like now.

When later they made love, it was no longer as strangers.

Nezemmut had gone to her cold bed long ago, though not without an assurance from her husband that he would visit her later, for the getting of an heir formed an important part of his busy schedule. In another part of the palace, in a large dark room overlooking the river on one side and the city to the north on the other, General Horemheb sat crouched at a black wood table on whose surface a number of scrolls were scattered.

Many were old, plundered long since from the archive at the City of the Horizon, because Horemheb was tracing his lineage. Before long, he thought, a time would come when his own historian would have to rewrite the annals of the Black Land in such a way as to make him the direct heir and successor of Nebmare Amenophis. Thus the difficult years of Akhenaten and his immediate successors would be erased for posterity, and even his own wife would cease to exist in the records. By then, if the gods were good, she would have served her purpose. For the moment, however, it was too soon to strike for the final goal. Patience had always been Horemheb's great ally; and he would not abandon his faith in it now, though age and time were not patient, and were beginning to nudge him.

For weeks he had not left the palace, brooding over the past, imagining the future, and leaving his men to control the present.

The reports he received were good, and he had no reason to think that their work was patchy. His belief in his own destiny had grown so hard that he could not imagine anything with the power to break it.

Kenamun stood near the table, half in the light cast by the lamps and half out of it. He bit his lip in impatience as he waited for his master to come down from the sky. They had got nothing out of Nehesy before they had killed him, and yet Horemheb's reaction to this news – Kenamun's chief dread – had been mild. Knowing the general's aversion to unnecessary torture, he had played down that part of the interrogation. In fear of betrayal, he had had the Medjay sergeant who had been present transferred to the Northern Capital – a move to which the sergeant himself had no objection. The vizir there was a quiet man who obeyed orders from the south. The place was no centre of power but merely the northern arm of the administration. It was a peaceful town, mainly concerned with trade and troop movements to and from the Delta.

'So, what would you advise?' Horemheb said finally.

'Ankhsenpaamun could pose a threat to the nation. If a core of resistance built up round her and there were civil war, some of our forces would have to be diverted from the Delta, and the risk of a Hittite invasion would be increased.' Kenamun chose his words carefully. Behind them was the simple message: kill the queen. But Kenamun knew that, as he progressed up the ladder of power, such brutal plain speaking had become increasingly abhorrent to the general. Indeed, his own old title was no longer pleasing to him, and he preferred these days to be known by the last of the many that he had prevailed upon Tutankhamun to bestow on him: Presider over the Two Lands, Great Lord of the People.

'But if the threat is removed before the burial of the pharaoh, will that not look displeasing? The priesthood is restless – they are conservative and adapt slowly; but I haven't the time to march at their pace.'

'The king's burial is still many weeks hence. The embalmers

will need another forty days to prepare him, and that is the one part of the process that cannot be hurried. Nor would it be seemly to do so.'

'Then we have an insoluble problem. For that time gives the queen an opportunity to organise.'

'Alone she is powerless.'

'But is she alone?'

'We believe her to be,' lied Kenamun, not wanting his own failure to infiltrate Ankhsenpaamun's household adequately to reach Horemheb's ears. The queen's intelligence service was better than he dared admit to the general, perhaps because it was so small and tightly-knit. Half the information he fed Horemheb on was invented.

'So there is no danger?' persisted the general.

'There is always danger in not making sure of a thing as soon as you can,' replied Kenamun cautiously. 'Especially if the stability of the Black Land is at stake. You rescued it after the fall of the Great Criminal. I do not want to see that work go for nothing.'

'But we have sealed all the cracks in our security.'

'Yes.'

'Whatever suspicions Horaha had have died with him.'

'Yes,' said Kenamun, more doubtfully. 'I still think I should interview the daughter.'

'She is not a danger,' said Horemheb loftily. 'What could she do? In any case we may safely leave her to Merinakhte. He is pleased with his reward for removing Horaha?'

'He seems to be.'

'Well, whether he is or not, he is our man now. He has bloodied his hands for us, and owes us house and career. Whether he can take the girl too – if he wants to – is his own affair. It does not affect us either way.'

Kenamun spread his hands. 'As you please. But what of Queen Ankhsenpaamun?'

Horemheb frowned. 'I will give her thought. But I do not see the urgency you seem to.'

'Be advised — '

Horemheb looked at him. 'I will seek advice when I need it,' he said, and turned back to his papers dismissively. Kenamun withdrew, but as soon as he was alone, Horemheb found that he could concentrate no longer. The hieroglyphs danced on the page, making no sense, and for no reason a chill shook him.

He kept seeing the queen's face in his heart. Kenamun's words stayed with him, and he was troubled.

# NINE

He had decided to visit her at the busiest time of day, when traders and servants were making their way to and from the pharaoh's palace, crowding the compound, chatting and bickering in its courtyards. Dressed in a shabby kilt, his beard unshaved, dirt from the riverbank rubbed on to his face, Huy's stocky figure disappeared in the mob of people. The difficulty was getting close to her, but the queen was expecting him, and once she had recognised him she had one of her body servants guide him through back corridors to a small room near the top of the building. There the man shaved Huy, applied make-up, and dressed his hair hastily, and gave him a clean tunic and kilt before leading him through the kitchens and then down through further corridors to another room, windowless and crammed with squat red columns, where he left him. No one who had seen the scruffy lighterman enter the palace would have associated him with the shaved and perfumed courtier who now stood waiting for Ankhsenpaamun.

She did not keep him waiting long, and when she arrived it was in haste. She swept aside formality, and he saw that though her face was worried, her eyes were clear.

'What is it?' he asked.

She looked at him. 'I have no doubt you know that my chief huntsman was arrested. They tell me he was plotting against me. Do you know what really happened?'

'He is dead,' said Huy. 'But I am sure that the last thing in his heart was betrayal.'

'I agree. But there is something else. My little sisters have been sent to the Northen Capital. Ay tells me it is for them to represent the *pschent* for the *Opet* festival there; but it is the first I have heard of the Northern Capital celebrating the *Opet* festival as well as here.'

'The net is closing,' said Huy.

'There is more still,' the queen continued, pacing up and down, hands fluttering, unable to stay still for a moment. 'Ay has repeated his request for a marriage.'

'What did you tell him?'

'I asked for time.'

'What did he say?'

'That I had none. He gave me five days.'

'And then?'

'Nothing. An empty threat.'

'What will you tell him when the time is up?'

'That I would rather die than marry him.'

Huy looked at her. 'You must leave the Southern Capital.'

'No. I will see my husband buried.'

'You owe it to him not to join him in the grave. It is not a responsibility that is yours alone any more. You carry a god within you.'

'A god should be able to take care of himself.'

'When they are in us they need help. Their power is limited by the frame they inhabit.'

The queen was silent, but she continued to look obstinate. 'Do not teach me my duty,' she said finally; and Huy knew that he had won.

'We must make plans quickly,' he said cautiously, after a pause.

'If I survive, and if I find that the king has not, after all, been given the full honour due to him, and if one day I have power to avenge the indignity, I will have horses drag you five times round the limits of the city,' she told him icily.

'There must be a boat. Not one of the falcon ships. I doubt if we could trust the sailors anyway,' said Huy, having shown her with his eyes that he had taken note of her threat.

'It is too much that I must flee my own city like a criminal,' she said. 'Perhaps if I consent to go – and not return – they will let me do so according to my rank.'

'No,' said Huy. 'They will not.'

'Ay is my own grandfather!'

'We must find a boat,' repeated Huy. 'In the hands of someone we can trust.'

'Who is there?' said the queen.

The embalmers had told Senseneb that her father would be ready for the great journey a month after the *Opet* festival – which still gave her fifty days in the house she had grown up in. Nevertheless, she had started to clear it, parting with most, regretfully bidding farewell to chairs, stools, papyrus rolls, tables, lamps, that she had known all her life. The things she could not bear to part with, Horaha's medical equipment; the little statue of Imhotep – her father's hero, the chief minister of the pharaoh Djoser and architect of the first great pyramid at Sakkara over a thousand years earlier; the images of the goddess Hathor, and of the gods Hor-Pa-Khred and Thoth, together with the best furniture and the most loved and important scrolls, she arranged to have shipped south to Napata. Although her future was uncertain, excitement and even pleasure had invaded the sadness and pessimism which had cast a shadow over her since her father's death. If she could not avenge it, she thought, she could perhaps at least vindicate his life. And perhaps – though this was a hope she did not dare bring fully into her heart yet – her own future would not now be as bleak as she had assumed. She tried not to let herself think about Huy, though already she had started to call him her brother to herself. Her winged heart flew away from her to him, and her body became strong and fluid, like the River, when he came into her thoughts.

Unconsciously, she had begun to take leave of the house already. Once a room was emptied, its character departed immediately, and it was as if it had never had anything to

122

do with her life, or only formed part of a half-remembered dream. Soon the whole place would be like that. What she would regret most would be the garden. Horaha and her mother had spent years creating it, and the medicinal herbs which grew there were thought by some to be the most important collection in the Black Land. As for the animals, the cats and the geese, Hapu's family would take them.

Senseneb was engaged in clearing a room when she saw Merinakhte standing in the doorway. She stopped what she was doing and looked at him, but said nothing, waiting for him to speak first. He held his body awkwardly, his grey eyes shifting uneasily.

'What are you doing?' he said at last.

She resumed her activity without answering.

'Don't you have servants to do that?'

'I have paid some off. Only Hapu is coming away with me. And there are things I like to do myself. In any case, you should be grateful.'

Merinakhte looked worried. 'It is not my fault that I have inherited your father's job.'

'No,' she replied evenly. 'It is very fortunate.'

Not catching her irony, he said earnestly, 'Perhaps it was something decreed by the gods.'

'Really?'

'Yes.' He pursued the idea eagerly. It seemed that now he had plucked up the courage to speak, the words would come tumbling out of him in a flood. 'Where are you going?'

For some reason her heart told her not to tell him. 'I haven't decided yet. Perhaps to the Northern Capital.'

'Doesn't your father have a house somewhere?'

'Who told you that?'

'He mentioned it once.'

'I haven't had time to go through all his papers.'

'I could help you.'

She looked at him. Everything about his body was too long, except his breast and thighs, which were flabby. His tiny eyes were like the points of spears in his pale face. He kept staring at a point below her waist, and his long fingers clasped and unclasped.

'No,' she said.

He was silent after that, but did not leave his position by the door. He tapped one of his feet up and down, twisting it in and out of his sandal in a manner so violent that for a moment she thought it must be uncontrollable.

She tried to ignore him, biting her lip, praying that he would go; but he stayed, staring. Where, she wondered, had Hapu got to? He had gone to take water for the garden out of the well with the *shaduf*, but he must have been finished by now.

It was becoming impossible for her even to pretend to work.

'What do you want?' she asked finally, straightening and looking at him. She found that she could not bear to for more than a few seconds together.

'You don't have to go,' he said, avoiding her eyes.

'What?'

'You don't have to go.' He allowed his eyes to meet hers briefly, to check how this comment had gone down, before they darted away again.

'There's nothing for me here any more.'

'There could be.'

She looked at him more carefully. He was trying to smile, achieving a sneer. His arms were folded defensively across his narrow chest, each bony hand grasping a pale forearm. He was like something that lived at the dark bottom of ponds, eating whatever sank there.

'What do you mean?' Her scalp crawled. A horrible realisation was coming into her heart.

'You could stay in this house. With me.' Now the words were out he seemed almost to regret having spoken them. One hand uneasily scratched its attendant forearm. She noticed that the nails were dirty and their pressure left a livid mark on the skin. Despite herself, she imagined that hand on her body, and felt the moisture of fear and disgust on her palms and forelip. But she had to say something. He was waiting for an answer.

'What?' she managed finally, hoping that she kept the incredulity out of her voice.

'With me. As my wife.' The hand detached itself from its anchor on his forearm and made an impotent, deprecating gesture in the air. For a ghastly moment she thought she might laugh. She managed to control the hysterical impulse. Above all she had to play safe.

'What about it? Will you be my wife?' blurted Merinakhte awkwardly.

'I need time – '

'I've had an eye on you for years. Ever since you came back here. I don't mind if you've been used once.'

Her eyes widened in anger. 'What?'

'I know why your husband sent you back. But children never appealed to me.'

Her head spun. 'I think you should leave.'

He folded his arms again, leaning insolently on the door frame. Now that he had embarked on his proposal, his assurance was growing. 'Not without an answer.'

'The answer is no.'

Merinakhte's lips tightened, and the veins at his temples pulsed. Then he controlled his anger, and whined, 'Please consider me, at least. Think, you could stay here. This would be your house. I'd let you do as you liked. You'd be mistress here. You could entertain my friends.'

'No.'

His eyes almost vanished into his face. 'If you leave this house, no one will look after your garden. Who will there be? I have no time for such things. It will have to be burned out and paved over.'

She looked at him. 'This is my house for another fifty days. You are trespassing in it. Leave now or I will have Hapu throw you out.'

He smiled nastily. 'Now, that *would* be a mistake.'

125

'Get out!'

He spread his hands. 'Just a moment, please. There is something else you might like to consider before you do that.'

She made herself breathe evenly. 'What is that?'

The unpleasant grin remained. 'I saw you. Thrashing around, grabbing each other. He took you like a dog takes a bitch.' The voice was quiet, but its edge was only just this side of insanity.

She looked at him, unable to speak.

'You and Huy. Oh yes, I know his name. What's your game with that little shit?'

'What —?'

'Or is he just servicing you? Must have built up, all those years without any.'

The fury broke over her like a wave, hollowing her stomach and making her head light. Immediately, cold calm followed. She knew without any doubt that as soon as it was possible she would kill this man, neatly and quickly.

He caught her thought and half laughed, half snarled. 'I'd come over to talk to you and I heard a noise. Like pigs rutting. I watched through the window. I was quiet, but I needn't have bothered. You two were so hard at it I could have walked through the room and you wouldn't have noticed.' He paused, letting the words sink in. 'But it doesn't matter. I'll still have you. I enjoyed watching. Who knows? If you like it I might set you at it with some of the servants now and then. I'm sure that'd be the kind of entertainment my friends would appreciate.'

'Why don't you crawl back under your stone?'

'I could have told Kenamun about you,' continued Merinakhte. 'It's probably my duty, especially if humping each other isn't all you are doing. But I love you, Senseneb, so I thought I'd be merciful. I'd do anything to keep you, my dear. And be sure of this. If I can't have you, no one else will.'

Again she could not answer. Her throat was too try to admit speech. Her *Ka* seemed to float above her. She watched the scene from outside herself as if it were a dream. She tried to send a thought from her heart to Huy, but the way was blocked.

There was a noise from beyond the room. Hapu was returning from the garden.

Merinakhte eased himself away from the door jamb. 'Think about what I have said. I am not a monster. But I will not wait long. I will be back for an answer soon.' He smiled. 'I am sure you will see sense. Despite the pleasures of the Fields of Aarru, we all prefer the short life we know to the eternity we do not.'

He left then, idly, not hurrying but not looking back. Senseneb's heart stampeded over possibilities. One thing was certain: Merinakhte was wrong. If she could not destroy him, she would prefer to risk Osiris's anger by killing herself than face a known hell on earth.

Huy had returned to his house to find Ineny waiting for him outside, idling among the handful of stallholders who set up a morning market twice a week in the little square. He greeted Huy brusquely, and hurried him towards the litter which was waiting to take them to Ay. For the second time that day, Huy set off for the palace compound. Huy noticed that Ineny was reserved once again. He was cordial, but no more than polite, and appeared disinclined to take the scribe into his confidence.

Huy did not have an opportunity to consider this return to reserve, as Ay was waiting for him in a greater state of agitation and impatience than Huy would have believed possible.

'You must tell me what you know now. *Now*!'

'I do not have the whole picture yet.'

'Never mind that!' Ay leant across the table between them, his arms trembling as they supported his body, his eyes showing white under the iris. 'I want all that you have got. I was a fool to let you have so much time.'

'What has happened?'

'Never mind. It does not concern you. An avenue has closed. That is all you need to know.'

Huy was aware of Ineny standing behind him, but could not turn to see his expression. Had Ay told him that the queen had rejected his marriage offer? Or was the humiliation so great that he had kept it to himself?

In the interval between his interview with Ankhsenpaamun and his meeting with Ay, Huy's heart, knowing that the last grains of sand were running through the clock with their usual and yet always unexpected rush, had constructed a plan which might cover all risks. It was a dirty plan, but it was no longer possible to fight in any other way and survive in the Black Land that was being created by this power struggle. Huy knew that the man to save the country was Horemheb; but the man to save the queen was still Ay, if he could be convinced that she was no threat to him. The way to achieve that was to ensure the throne for the old man. If, later, destiny decreed that Horemheb should succeed him, then destiny would be helped greatly by nature, for Ay was old and without a direct heir. Horemheb, too, was not the kind of man to be cast down by frustration and defeat; rather, they would make him roar the louder. For himself, he hoped for nothing more than to be far away from the city, soon, and, despite all the warnings and reservations that rose in his heart, with Senseneb.

'Very well, if you wish it,' he told Ay after a pause.

'Good.' Ay leant forward.

'Before I begin, there are conditions.'

Ay pushed himself back off the table and paced to and fro three or four times. After controlling himself, he turned again to Huy.

'Conditions?' he asked. His tone was low, but his voice was strained.

'Yes.' Huy was also struggling to keep his voice soft, and diplomatically neutral. He did not want to betray the strain he was putting his own courage under. He wished that there were another way out, but he could see none.

'What are they?'

Huy was still aware of Ineny at his back. His mouth was dry.

'I want you to guarantee the safety of Queen Ankhsenpaamun.'

Ay involuntarily spread his hands, almost surprised. 'Is that all?'

'No, but it is important.'

'I will assure her of my personal protection, without reservation.' Ay looked at him, and Huy could tell from his eyes that he knew he was not believed.

'You will also have to drop all thoughts of marrying her.'

Ay reddened. 'What?'

'I cannot take your word alone as sufficient guarantee of her safety.'

'How dare —?'

'Let us be realistic. I need to be able to take her away from here, to a place of safety, where she will not be molested by you or by Horemheb. I need your help to get her away. In return, I can give you enough damaging information concerning Horemheb's activities to ensure that, once he knows you have it, he will not contest your claim to the Golden Chair.'

'No information is that good.'

'This is. The general would never hold the priesthood or the army together if it became open knowledge. No pharaoh yet has held power who has shown himself to be more of a man than a god, and Horemheb is not heaven-born.' The last remark went home to Ay, himself a commoner, as it was intended to.

'I will be generous,' said Ay graciously, after a short pause for form's sake. 'Now, tell me what you know.'

Behind him, Huy heard a faint rustling and the scrape of a chair. Ineny had brought out a scribe's palette and a scroll.

'There is something else first,' he said. 'The queen is concerned about Nebkheprure Tutankhamun's journey to the west.'

Ay spread his hands again. 'He will be given a burial worthy of a great pharaoh. I am in charge of the arrangements myself.'

'Good.' Huy thought of the poor funeral furniture he had seen and wondered if Ay would better it. It seemed unlikely, but there was no time to bargain details. 'Then there is another entombment.'

Ay looked at him: 'Whose?'

'The doctor, Horaha's.'

'His position guarantees him one.'

'There may be no one to watch over him. He must be given a formal burial in full accordance with his rank, and all his names must be written down over the lintel and in the chapel. This must not be left to his successor.'

'You have my word,' snapped Ay impatiently. 'But of what importance is Horaha now?'

'You will hear.'

Ay sat down. Behind him, the sun streamed over the city and the swelling river, making a silhouette out of the old man. He sat still as rock while Huy spoke, his head lowered on to his hands. The silence was broken only by the soft swish of Ineny's brush as he wrote. Huy told him of the king's death, of his meeting with Nehesy, about finding the dead tracker with his fistful of silver; about the uninjured horses, and about what Horaha had thought about the king's injuries. Finally he told him about Horaha's death, and Nehesy's arrest and torture. He did not mention where Nehesy was now. The man deserved his peace.

'Even the threat of an inquiry in any of those areas would stop Horemheb in his tracks,' said Ay, when Huy had finished. He looked at him. 'You have done well. But I need proof.'

'Horaha's reservations can be demonstrated.'

'How?'

'The king's body is being preserved. No one can disguise the wound on the skull now. If you can lay hands on the chariot, you have a case. But I think all you need do is mention that to Horemheb. You are too powerful for him to destroy; and he cannot kill everyone.'

'I wonder,' said Ay.

'I mean, he has not that much power. But then there is me.'

In the act of rising, Ay looked at him again and sat down. 'You?'

'I collected these facts and have a record of them. I am still alive.'

'Yes?'

Huy hesitated fractionally before continuing. 'Forgive me, but I cannot trust you absolutely. Now you have what you need, I run the risk of becoming dispensable – I, and all that I seek as a reward.'

'Your conditions?'

'Yes.'

'They make an easy reward to grant. And I give you my word as pharaoh-elect.' Ay seemed to grow physically as he spoke the words. The new thought occurring to his heart threw years off the lined face. 'You are lucky that I am pleased with you. I am not offended by what you say. But do not try me too hard.'

'I know that you are a wise man. Therefore I know too that you are aware of the threat that the queen's life, and the one within her, pose to the future of your line.' Huy paused. 'I must tell you that if I find myself crossed in any way, I will go to Horemheb and warn him. If anything happens to me, the record I have made of these events will go to him. It is safe, in a place you will never locate, and I have made arrangements with friends in the harbour quarter who are such little eels that they will always wriggle through your fingers if you attempt to catch them. But they have strong jaws.' Privately, Huy wished that he had indeed made such a record.

Ay turned in on himself, the fingers of each hand touching one another at the tips. His face was turned downwards, and it was impossible to see the expression on his face.

'Do you have a plan for the queen's departure?'

'Of sorts.'

'But have you considered Horemheb? You might have to trust me, for all your skill; but if Horemheb thinks that she

131

is alive – wherever she is in the Black Land – he will not rest until he has hunted her down and killed her. *And* her child. He has the means to do it, too, Huy. Even if I beat him now, I cannot strip him of his power without risking a division of the army. And we cannot have that.'

'I have thought of what to do.' In reality, Huy had only the sketchiest of plans, and a weak and dangerous one.

Ay smiled. 'I have often said that you were a clever man, Huy.' He paused delicately. 'I suppose it is a waste of time to offer you land when I become pharaoh? In return for your service, of course.'

'Yes.'

Ay pursed his lips. 'Then you shall have your wish. Ineny will escort you to the gate.' He stood up. Ineny packed up his palette and prepared to stow the rolled parchment under his arm.

'Leave that with me, Ineny,' said the old Master of Horse.

She was not at their meeting place. Huy squatted down on the flat rock which jutted out forming a ledge over the surface of the River and watched the sluggish, patient water pass. Idling the time away with his thoughts at first, for he was early and felt no alarm, he let his heart drift with the current as it proceeded on its eternal journey north, knowing that this water *was* the Black Land; that it would flow here long after the pyramids had crumbled to dust and even the memory of them been lost. What was happening now, what seemed of such monumental importance to him and to his own little life, would not affect the future one iota. He thought as far ahead as his imagination would run. Perhaps there were more countries, even beyond those bordering the Great Green to the north and the forests far to the south. Was there life in those countries? Would they, too, one day be discovered, visited, colonised?

Such considerations made him wince. They did not matter to him. He might only be a speck in the scheme of time and space, but the immediate world to which he was condemned surrounded him with matters whose reality and importance could not be reduced just by thinking about them in relative terms. An attacking lion was an attacking lion, no matter how little time and space its action occupied.

The sun dipped over the western horizon and at last Huy felt the coolness of the north wind on his face. He blinked his tired eyes slowly, gratefully. But he did not relax. Senseneb was late now. He settled himself with his back to another rock and, instead of simply continuing to wait, kept watch. His apparent victory with Ay by no means meant that the game was over.

Darkness descended suddenly, and immediately the small, pale lights that mankind lit to keep it at bay appeared on both banks of the River. The flat rock stood at a point just to the south of the city where few people passed at night. Senseneb would have been here before sunset if she was coming at all. Still he waited, though now he knew that it was in vain. After half an hour he stood up, and, still uncertain what to do, made his way back to the city.

By the time he had reached the outskirts he had decided to risk going to her house. In his heart he ran over what the possibilities might be, raking through his memory for any sin of omission or commission which might have led to this. He told himself that it might be nothing at all even though he knew that now any mistake, any irregularity, any broken promise, however small, was not only important but vital.

As he walked through the already deserted streets he began to have second thoughts about visiting Senseneb. It was necessary to keep her out of this, he said to himself. But another part of his heart was desperate to know what had happened to her. The streets were dark, only punctuated by the occasional pale shaft of light from a window where a lamp shone, though the moon was still bright enough to illuminate the middle of the broadest roads. Khons's chariot had not yet turned so far away from the earth that only a sliver of it could be seen at night.

133

He walked where the moonlight met the shadow, moving as softly as a cat. The few people he encountered walked past quickly, just allowing eyes to meet briefly for reassurance. Here and there on a corner a drinking house splashed more light, but the windows were small, and the sound from within was muted.

Making his way across the city he had to pass through the harbour quarter. It occurred to him quite irrationally that Senseneb might have gone to his house, so he turned down the side street which led to his little square. The street was narrow and plunged into deep shadow; Huy had not walked twelve paces down it before a hand reached out and grasped his right arm. He stopped dead and reached behind him with his left hand for his knife, but her voice arrested his action.

'Huy.' Senseneb's face emerged from the darkness like the moon from behind a cloud.

Before he could ask questions she put a finger to her lips and led him back the way they had come. She seemed to know her way through the twisting streets of the quarter as well as he did. After a short time they arrived at the quayside. They stopped by a warehouse wall from where they had a broad view of every approach.

'What's happened?' asked Huy, keeping his voice low. He was disturbed at how tightly Senseneb held on to his arm, as a child might, returned to its parent after a beating. Calmly, deliberately, but making a visible effort to keep her voice steady, she told him.

'I didn't dare come to meet you in case he followed me. So I went out several times on false errands and returned home. Then I left again and took a rickshaw. I came down to the centre, to the Great Temple of Amun, and got off there. I was so scared I thought at first that I'd bring Hapu with me; but then I thought it'd be better to leave him to guard the house. As soon as I'd made sure Merinakhte hadn't followed me I went down to the harbour quarter and hid in that street, where I could see the square and your house. I don't think anyone paid much attention to me, though one man stopped and offered me two *deben* of copper to go with him. I told him I was worth twice that, and he left.' She laughed, but then almost immediately started to cry, softly but painfully, turning her face to Huy, nestling up to him and cradling herself in his arms. He held her gently, saying nothing.

At length she was quiet. The *kohl* around her eyes had run with her tears and he dabbed at it with a fold of his shawl, eliciting a smile again.

'What shall we do?'

'No one is going to betray you to Kenamun,' said Huy, 'but you must go back home.'

'No!'

'It will not be for long. How much have you told Hapu?'

'He knows that Merinakhte is not welcome. He hates him anyway. That house was as much Hapu's home as mine.'

'Whatever happens, Hapu must stay there. You must not make it look as if you are leaving.' He held up his hand as she opened her mouth to object. 'It is all right. We will be able to make arrangements for Hapu to follow us after we are gone, if he wishes it.'

'And when will that be?'

'Soon.'

'But my father – '

Huy looked at her. 'There is no time to talk of that now. But do not worry. I will come to you soon. I will take every precaution. I must arrange for the queen's departure. Ay has agreed to it but I must move fast in case he changes his mind.'

'Can I help you?'

'Your help will be vital, if all goes well. But not yet.' He made a move to go.

'Huy.' She touched his lips with her fingers.

'Be brave.'

'I am terrified.'

'So am I.'

135

They smiled at each other, touched foreheads, and kissed. 'Now go,' he said.

As Senseneb drew away from Huy and hurried into the night, Horemheb, in the low dark workroom of his palace, angrily crushed a document in one large fist and glared up at the two men who stood opposite him. Illuminated from below by the lamps on the table, they looked like demons. One wore an expression of uneasy pleasure. The other looked taut, and angry.

'What Ineny has just told us is very interesting,' Horemheb said, turning from Ay's servant to Kenamun. 'It makes me wonder what our people have been doing. From your reports I thought that everything was in order.'

'It is. This is a new development, but not unexpected.' Kenamun ran his tongue over his lips. Huy again. He had not forgotten their encounter years earlier, and his regret was that he had not finished him then. His misguided gratitude for the little scribe's help in solving a case was rebounding on him now.

'This man Huy is a former servant of the Great Criminal,' put in Ineny.

'Yes,' replied Horemheb. 'I met him once myself. We have underestimated him.'

'He is nobody,' said Kenamun.

'Is he? He has managed to be a thorn in our side.'

'I know where he lives. I'll deal with him,' said Kenamun, eager to recover lost ground.

'Be careful,' said Ineny. 'He is under Ay's protection.'

Kenamun looked at him with contempt. Horemheb ignored them both, retreating into his thoughts. Ineny's information had come too late. If the man had decided to change sides earlier, things might have been different. He smoothed out the paper he had crumpled. It was a summons from Ay to a meeting, to be attended by the chief priest of Amun and the vizir of the Southern Land, the following morning. That

Ay should suddenly have the assurance to *summon* him to a meeting was a shock. His shoulders slumped. At least he had the advantage of knowing what to expect. They might be able to block him, but they could not destroy him. And if it meant that he had to let Ay wear the *pschent* and become pharaoh, what then? He had ten years on the old man, and Nezemmut was young. She would have more children.

Still he could have done without this. He looked up at the two greedy, sullen, expectant faces above him. A pair of Set's vampires, and worth about as much. Perhaps he had used the wrong tools to climb with.

Irresistibly, his thoughts turned to the armies in the north. He had always been more of a soldier than a politician. He would see what could be salvaged from the wreck. In the meantime . . .

Pointing at Ineny he looked at Kenamun. 'Pay this shit off and get Huy,' he said. 'Now. Tonight. Yourself.'

He rose and crossed to the window, dismissing them with his back. A petty revenge, killing Huy. Like stamping on a scorpion after it had stung you. He heard the men leave the room, the hasty scuffle of their feet on the floor. But if Huy killed Kenamun, that would be no loss. Kenamun had ceased to be useful now.

After leaving Senseneb, Huy returned to his house, but he did not stay long. He washed and changed quickly, filled his purse, and made his way quickly down the street to another square. This was almost as empty as the one on which he lived; but on one corner there was a dingy drinking house, and in the middle of the wall opposite was a low entrance with a sign above it lit by an oil lamp: City of Dreams. It was a brothel, a familiar place which he had occasionally used, along with the rivermen, tradesmen and craftsmen who lived in the harbour quarter. It was run by a fat Nubian called Nubenehem who had grown so large that she was virtually incapable of moving from the couch she inhabited behind the low table from which she conducted her affairs in the entrance of the house. The dimly-lit room was dominated these days by a statue of the god Min, adorned with an erection of prodigious length and width.

Nubenehem was more than a friend. She had been Huy's accomplice, provider and, now and then, confessor. But he had never begged a favour like the one he asked now.

The idea seemed ramshackle, even to him; but with Senseneb's medical skill, and Nubenehem's limitless contacts in the harbour quarter, it might work.

The fat Nubian was dealing with a client, a spindly young man who stood by nervously while his equally spindly father negotiated for a girl to initiate his son. When the youth saw Huy he turned away and studied the wall behind him with great attention.

His father was trying to beat Nubenehem's price down.

'But you want a good girl,' she was saying. 'By the gods, if you set him off with a cut-rate one, what kind of impression is he going to have of women?'

'I won't pay more than one *piece*.'

She spread her hands, a comical expression of distress covering her suffocating features. 'We don't have any girls for under one *kitë*. That's our lowest rate.' She appeared to consider, catching Huy's eye. 'Look, I'll tell you what we could do. Little Kafy is between clients – well, she's not so little these days, but she's had plenty of experience – and I could let him have her for half an hour now for one and a half *kitë* of silver. The gentleman who's just come in knows her. He'll vouch for her.'

After the matter had been settled and Kafy had been summoned for the father's approval, draping her ample body round the apprehensive boy before leading him off, with his watchful father in attendance, into the brothel's interior, Nubenehem turned to Huy.

'Do I recognise you?'

'A moment ago you did.'

'Huy.'

'Am I that much of a stranger?'

'If all my clients were like you I wouldn't be here any more.'

'I'm here to ask you something.'

'I'm relieved. For just a moment I thought you might have missed me. Did you see how fat Kafy's become? She eats to console herself. She misses you.'

'Will you help me?'

Nubenehem gave him what passed for a smile: the folds around her mouth arranged themselves more comfortably. 'You know me. If you pay me, I'll help you.'

Huy licked his lips.

'That difficult, is it?' asked Nubenehem.

'I need a body.'

'What?'

'A corpse. A girl's dead body.'

Nubenehem half rose, despite herself. 'Now I know you've gone mad.'

'Can you get one?'

'No.'

'It is very important.'

Nubenehem looked at him. 'I can get you all the live girls you want. But when they're dead, they need a little peace.'

'This one will have peace. She will get a better burial than she would ever have dreamed of, and her *Ka* will live in the valley.'

Now Nubenehem sat up. '*What*?'

'I need a dead body,' repeated Huy. 'A girl who looks like Queen Ankhsenpaamun. Have you seen her? Do you know what she looks like?'

'I have seen her. But what you are asking is impossible. Sure people die, young people die, young girls die; but not to order. When do you need it anyway?'

'Now.'

'Be serious.'

'Within the next two days.'

'I asked you to be serious.'

'She need not be identical. People change in death. But she must bear a good passing resemblance. So that with make-up we can disguise her as the queen.'

Nubenehem said nothing for a moment. She looked inwards. From the depths of the house beyond came a burst of music, played badly on a lute, and a theatrical squeal of pleasure.

'What are you doing, Huy?'

'I cannot tell you, and you would not want to know.'

'You are right, I would not.' She paused again. 'Are you sure you are not flying too high at last?'

'It is like being a child on a swing,' he replied. 'It goes up and up, forwards and back, and usually when it is too high you can stop it by ceasing to use your body as a pendulum. The swing that I am on has its ropes attached to the sky, and it has pulled me further and further, higher and higher, until I can look down and see the whole earth beneath me. And I cannot stop it, Nubenehem. All I can do to get back to safety is jump off.'

'And break your neck?'

'There is that risk. But there is no choice.'

Nubenehem was silent again, but not for long.

'I will help you.' For a moment Huy thought her look was sympathetic; but then the craftiness crept back into her eyes. 'It will cost you plenty; I have no idea if I can find what you want, and I do not know what excuse I can find to stop tongues blabbing. Fortunately in this part of town death is frequent and the population shifts.' She looked up at him. 'I need some money now.'

Huy opened his purse. 'How much?'

Once he had concluded his business, he crossed the square quickly to the drinking house and ordered a jar of fig liquor and a bowl of sunflower seeds. He found a place on a bench and squeezed into it, his back to the wall, looking round the small plain room at his companions. They were all locals, some

140

of them known to him, and he had lived in the quarter long enough not to be an object of curiosity for them.

He also needed to think about how he was going to finance the queen's escape without her co-operation. He doubted if Ay would underwrite the hire of a boat and Nubenehem's fee completely. He drank some of the liquor. It was poorly made and scorched his throat. Perhaps he would have to take Ay further into his confidence.

Much later, and still uncertain, he made his way back to his house.

He had reached the edge of the square before he realised that something was wrong. He stood still, in the shadow of the nearest building. Some of the market traders had not dismantled their tumbledown stalls, and he looked in their direction. From a bundle of abandoned sacking which had contained fruit, first the snout and then the body of a large black rat emerged. Satisfied that all was well, it waddled across the centre of the square. Huy followed it with his eyes until it disappeared into the shadow of the opposite wall. Still Huy waited, alert as a fox in open desert, but nothing moved.

Finally, he started on his way again, but, lacking the assurance of the rat, he skirted the walls until he reached his door. There was still nothing, and there was nothing when he went in; but his unease did not leave him. Quietly he climbed the narrow steps that led up to the bedroom, but everything was as he had left it. He descended again and made his way through the main room to the bathroom at the back, where he saw that he had not refilled the wooden water bucket. The room, and the small courtyard at the back, were deserted.

He returned to the front of the house, but he had begun to relax, and he did not see the knife soon enough. It sliced upwards, cutting his cheek to the bone, which stopped the blade just below his left eye. Gasping, he pulled backwards, aware how the liquor had slowed him. Blood filled his mouth and he choked on it. His eyes watered so that he could not focus on the lean figure in front of him.

141

'Hello, Huy,' said Kenamun. The knife plunged forwards again, but Huy managed to shrink back and it cut air.

'You shit; you nearly destroyed me,' said Kenamun, breathing hard. Huy noticed that, and wondered how fit the man was. His actions were fast enough, certainly. He tried to reply, but the blood that kept pouring into his mouth would not let him. He risked drowning in it, he knew. He made himself breathe through his nose but the knife had cut into the back of it and now his nostrils filled with blood too. He spat out a beakerful and gulped air.

Kenamun must have seen what a mess his victim was in because he relaxed, straightening and holding the knife slack. He pushed Huy gently in the chest with the flat of his hand. Huy staggered back a pace into the bathroom, but kept his balance.

'You are dying,' said Kenamun. He pushed Huy again, harder. Spitting and gulping, Huy fell back against the wall, his arms sprawling, his hands grabbing for support as he slid to the floor.

Kenamun leant over him. Huy could see the grinning face, the pencil beard, through a haze of blood. 'I think you have been getting ideas above your station, Huy,' he said. 'If Ay's fat little servant hadn't got greedy your little bit of palace intrigue would have cost me my neck. It's all right now, that's why I'm here; I've been sent to kill you. But first I think you need cutting down to size.'

The fingers of Huy's right hand had found the handle of the wooden bucket. If he had remembered to fill it it would have been too heavy to lift. Realising that Kenamun was enjoying his moment too much, he filled his lungs with one more large breath for the effort and lifted the bucket, hurling it through the air at the end of his arm. Its copper-bound side caught Kenamun on the side of the head and Huy heard bone split. He felt rather than saw the man fall, and heard the clatter of the knife as it hit the stone bathing platform. Blood filled his universe. He struck out blindly, defensively, as he brought himself to his knees, but connected with nothing but the air. Crawling forwards, not losing his grip on the bucket, he reached out with his left hand in the direction he had sensed Kenamun fall.

He felt the cloth of his robe and then he had his hand on the man's chest. Kenamun rolled out of his reach. He raised himself on to his knees, slipping on his own blood. Below him he could just focus on a long object, like a rolled rug, which rocked to and fro, to and fro. He raised the bucket above his head and brought it crashing down with all his force, gasping and gagging on the blood which continued to bubble into his mouth and choke his nostrils. Recovering his balance, he panicked, for he could not see the body. Had Kenamun got up? Reached the knife?

He made his eyes focus, searching the floor, dragging the bucket with him as he pulled himself forward. There he was. He had rolled out of reach again, that was all. He tried to decide which end the head was. Objects swam in front of his streaming vision; water and blood obscured it. Suddenly he was aware of fingers reaching towards his eyes. One of Kenamun's hands clawed into the wound in Huy's cheek and gripped. He raised the bucket again, and smashed it down, thinking, this is for Nehesy, but also feeling, this is for myself. You must die. I must be sure you are dead. I fear you too much. The bucket hit the ground, and jarred out of his hand. He heard the wood splinter. Frantic, he scrambled after it, seized it, and raised it again. This time it hit home and Kenamun's body, after one convulsion and a long rattling sigh which was the only sound it had made since it first fell, lay still.

# TEN

She bathed off the caked blood and cleaned the ripped flesh, throwing the linen wad which Huy had used to staunch the blood into the fire. She looked at the wound and, as he sat still, passively, he looked at her. She caught his eye briefly and smiled.

'It's a filthy mess. I'm going to put something on it which will hurt, and then you must drink three cups of flame liquor because it will hurt more when I stitch it up and I want you to keep still. I'll do my best but you will always have a scar there.'

She turned to the fire, over which herbs were simmering in a copper pot. Through the door open to the garden, he could see Hapu picking chervil, coriander and dill. The two *ro* geese, taking a morning walk, came into view and peered inside inquisitively. He sat at a plain sycamore-wood table. It was a high-ceilinged room, whitewashed, bare of decoration. Against the wall opposite the fireplace stood a hard couch, above which pots, retorts and bronze implements were ranged on shelves. This had been Horaha's consulting room, and it was here that she had brought him immediately after his arrival in the ninth hour of night.

She had not yet asked him for any explanation, and Huy was too exhausted to give any. He was happy to surrender to Senseneb's skilled attention, and he was grateful for her restraint.

The lamp on the table was still lit, though by now the sun had risen fully. Huy wondered how long Horemheb would wait for Kenamun to report back before sending someone to look for him. He thought of the police chief's smashed body, still lying spreadeagled in the bathroom of his house. He had covered it with a blanket before leaving, but he had not had the strength to do more otherwise than close and bolt his doors. He had known that if he could not get medical help quickly he would collapse, and instinctively he had come to Senseneb, leaving immediately in order to arrive before dawn.

She took the bowl off the fire and placed it on the table, dipped a soft cloth into it and turned to him again. The liquid gave off a pungent, unpleasant odour.

'Now,' she said. 'Be brave.'

The boiling water seared the flesh at first, and the effect of the potion was a harsh stinging that ran outwards from his wound across his face; but it was followed by a numbness that brought relief.

'All right?'

'Yes.'

'Good. Now for the difficult part.' She smiled encouragement at him. No word had been said, but each of them had laid aside the last reservations they had had about each another and now they basked, like lizards in the sun, in the confidence of their hearts. He saw himself in her eyes as she saw herself in his.

She brought the liquor and placed it by him with a cup. Turning, she called Hapu, who came in, and, smiling at Huy, took up a position behind the chair.

'What about Merinakhte?' asked Huy.

Senseneb looked grim. 'He hasn't been back. But Hapu has kept the outer gates locked, and today he will be at the House of Healing. He has already taken up my father's duties.'

'I am sorry for his patients.'

She looked at him. 'Don't be. He is a doctor of great talent. In some way his *Ka* is torn down the middle.'

'He is a dangerous man.'

'Yes. Now, drink the three cups of liquor. That will be enough to deaden the pain. When I start, I will work

145

quickly. Grip the sides of the chair tightly. Hapu will hold you still. Trust him. It will not take long. Would you like us to blindfold you?'

'No.' But Huy felt a qualm at the back of his heart.

She turned to a smaller copper vessel on the fire. Bringing it to the table, she washed her hands and then, taking off its lid, took a thin needle from it, which she threaded from a bobbin of gut. Huy drank the liquor. It burned his throat and stomach, leaving its familiar glow behind. Huy was in the habit of drinking more than he should, and he worried that three cups would not be enough, but by the time he had tipped back the third his head swam. He felt Hapu pin him to the back of the chair, and dutifully grasped its sides with his hands.

Senseneb came close, and placed the fingers of one hand on his cheek, either side of the wound. In the other she held the needle. It was very near his eye.

'Now,' she said gently.

She worked fast, as she had promised, and the darting pain of the needle as it passed through the flesh was over almost before it began. When the job was finished, she stood back, looking at her handiwork.

'Good,' she said, handing him a bronze mirror. He looked at the wound. It was livid, and the criss-cross of stitches made him look like a child's drawing of a river pirate, but his face was recognisably his own once more.

'Now you must rest.'

'No.'

'You don't have a choice.'

'There isn't time.'

She cleaned his cheek with water. 'You must make time. You can pass it by telling me what happened. I might have died of fright when you arrived here.'

He told her and she listened gravely.

'There is something else,' said Huy, finishing.

'What?'

146

'I am arranging for Queen Ankhsenpaamun to leave within days. I want you to go with her.'

'Where?'

'To the south. I would like you to take her to Napata.'

She frowned. 'I will not leave here until I have seen my father buried. I have told you. And I will not leave without you.'

He held her arms. 'The longer you stay, the greater the danger.'

'Kenamun is dead.'

'Yes. And it cannot be concealed long. When it is discovered, who knows what will happen?'

She was silent.

'I have spoken to Ay,' said Huy. 'He guarantees your father's burial and the care of his *Ka*.'

'Do you believe that he will keep his word?'

'If he gets the Golden Chair, there will be no reason for him to act dishonourably.'

She smiled. 'Your faith is touching.'

'No. He will want to make a good impression on the people. Horaha was a loyal servant of Tutankhamun. Do not forget the dead are with us always. They watch.'

'Do you believe that?'

Huy looked away. 'It is not a question of what I believe, but of what is accepted.'

'And what will you be doing, while I am escorting the queen to Napata?'

'Making sure you are not followed.'

She took his face in her hands so he could not look away. 'You are not getting rid of me, are you?'

'What does your heart tell you?'

She looked down, letting go of his face.

'What you ask is much.'

'The risks are great whether we stay or go. The rewards are greater if we go.'

The morning was far advanced when he made his way across

147

the palace compound to visit Ay. This was the first time he had come unannounced, and he was cautious in case Ineny was there. But if Kenamun's body had not been discovered, Ineny would have no idea that Huy was aware of his treachery. Another risk that had to be taken.

He made his way to a side entrance, displayed his badge of office to the guard, and was admitted; but the house servant who greeted him told him that Ay was meeting with Horemheb and the high dignitaries of the city, and put him in an airless antechamber to wait. There was nothing else for Huy to do.

When he received him, Ay was in a contented mood. Huy had not had to wait long, though half an hour had been an age, and the sun beyond the window of the antechamber had seemed to hang without movement in the sky.

'We meet sooner than I had expected,' said the old man. 'Is there trouble?'

'Yes.'

Ay was alert, but the smile did not leave his lips. 'I imagine we can deal with it. What has happened?'

'First of all, I must have your confidence.'

Ay continued to smile. 'That you already have. And my gratitude. We are alone. No one is hiding in the shadows. Speak freely.'

'Ineny has betrayed you to Horemheb.'

The Master of Horse did not look surprised. 'If he has, he is too late.' He leant forward. 'I thought about your threats to go to Horemheb yourself if I did not do as you requested. So I decided not to wait for that, but to tell him myself. Of course it was necessary to create certain ... embellishments, but he sees how things are.' He drew himself up. 'You must be quick. I have little time. There is much to prepare.'

'For what?'

'For taking the Golden Chair. You are looking at the next pharaoh.'

Huy was silent for a moment, then smiled. 'You never believed in the force of my threat, did you?'

'I knew you had given me enough to hang Horemheb, provided that I acted fast.' Ay's smile had faded.

'So you stole a march on me.'

'Yes. You are a clever man, Huy, as I have said more often than I care to remember. But even Horus has only one eye, so how can a mere man be blamed for a blind spot? I secured the king's chariot and his horses; I sent men men to recover the tracker's body; I sealed off the huntsmen's quarters and interned the men themselves. I can strike fast when I need to. People think that because I am old, and proceed with care, that I cannot move when I want to; but no cobra was ever swifter than me. And you gave me all I needed.'

'All power to you, Kheperkheprure Ay.' Inwardly, Huy was congratulating himself that he had delayed telling Ay anything for so long.

The old man smiled again, but his eyes were hooded. 'Tell me about Ineny. How did you learn about him?'

'Through Kenamun. Horemheb sent him to kill me last night.'

The pharaoh-elect raised his eyebrows. 'And where is Kenamun now.'

'At my house.'

'Dead?'

'Yes.'

'By the look of your face he almost got you.'

'I saw the sail of the Boat of the Night.'

Ay looked out of the window at the sun. 'He must be moved soon.'

'Yes.'

'Don't worry about Horemheb. He has too much to think about to worry about a lost *senet* piece like Kenamun. But he does not like loose ends.'

'That is why I came here. For your help.'

'What makes you think I will give it?'

Huy spread his hands. 'You have what you want.'

Ay laughed drily. 'Yes, I do. And something tells me to

keep on the right side of you, Huy. Won't you really join me?' The old man paused. 'You could be senior scribe, here in the palace compound. Would that appeal to you? Keeper of the royal archive, for example?'

Huy's heart ached, but the decision was no longer his to make. Certainly not now; and he did not foresee a long reign for the man who stood opposite him.

'You are generous. But I have a job to finish.'

Ay waved his hand. 'Ah yes. Little Ankhsi. Well, take her away if you must. She will not be a danger to me, and we have had enough bloodshed. But do not forget Horemheb. I am not so naive as to think he is beaten for good. If you want my help, you must tell me what you are going to do.'

'And Kenamun?'

'Leave him to me. Do not go back to your house tonight. By morning only the memory of his visit will remain.'


Huy spent much of the day down by the harbour. His wound throbbed, but he had no mirror to see what it looked like, and he had no intention of returning to Senseneb. Here, although he drew a few glances, people were too busy to pay much attention to him as he joined the usual bunch of quayside loafers watching the barges loading and unloading. Wide cedar barges from the northern country east of the Great Green, where the trees grew; gold carriers from the south. Limestone from the north, sandstone and granite from the First Cataract.

Three falcon ships were loading a regiment to head north to the Delta. Couriers had brought news that a Hittite army was gathering and rumours had its destination as the northern desert. The soldiers were conscripts – young, dusty and apprehensive, peasant boys who everyone hoped would be back by the time the flood had subsided, to work the black silt at the beginning of *peret*.

Huy searched among the ships for one belonging to Taheb's fleet, but he did not see one, or a single face he knew. The day passed slowly, but there would be no point in visiting Nubenehem until the evening. Then, if she had been successful in fulfilling Huy's request, everything would have to move quickly. Although Ay had reacted to Huy's plan with scepticism, he had not dismissed it out of hand. Huy would not be forced to stage manage the whole thing on his own now, and his appeal for funds had not been rejected; but Ay had outmanoeuvred him, and he still could not bring himself to trust his new and enforced ally completely.

At last the shadows lengthened and the sun lost its heat, turning a deep red and growing as it always did when it approached the daily moment of its death, dipping with emerald flashes below the edge of the world to warm the empire of Osiris below. The crowd of porters and tradesmen, hawkers and longshoremen, sailors and idlers, dispersed quickly to their homes or to the eating and drinking houses whose owners were already lighting the sparse lamps hanging from mud brick walls. Huy made his way up the sloping street that led to the alleyways of the harbour quarter, and reached the door of the City of Dreams just as dusk was ceding the palm to night.

Nubenehem looked up as he entered. He could tell at once that she had no good news for him.

'What did you expect?' she said. 'It was a crazy idea.'

'There's still time.'

Nubenehem laughed. 'Not a chance. I've already asked around – and that kind of request makes people ask questions. If you want to keep whatever it is you're up to a secret, then don't ask me for help.' She paused for a moment. 'And there's no refund.'

'Give it one more try. There's still a day.'

'I'm not sticking my neck out any further.' The fat woman's face was closed. 'The way things are going in this town, it is bad business to do favours, even little ones, for friends.'

'You took the silver quickly enough.'

Nubenehem glared at him. 'I'm not Hathor. I can't help you.'

Huy left. His heart was racing, but he told himself that the

151

idea had been too dependent on chance in the first place. He would have to get Ankhsenpaamun out without faking her death, and take the chances of pursuit. He made his way to his house cautiously and watched it from a distance but it, and the square, were deserted. He could not go to Senseneb, for he did not know if Merinakhte would be keeping watch. He thought of Taheb, but quickly rejected the idea. Facing a fact that he had long been aware of, but avoided, that the kind of life he led made his existence friendless, he turned back to the harbour, and the lights of the drinking houses.

At dawn Ineny stood in his master's workroom, thinking about the narrow escape he had had. Though he had long since stowed the leather bag of gold which Kenamun had given him so contemptuously, his hand still remembered its weight. The humiliation had stung him, but what horrified him most was the thought of the risk he had taken. He sweated with relief at the balancing thought, that he had got away with it, and was still on the winning side. Kenamun was dead. Horemheb had better things to do than betray him to Ay, but had shown no sign that he wished to buy him over to his side. Ineny now thought of the man whom, only hours earlier, he had tried to destroy, with warmth and gratitude. Once Ay was pharaoh what avenues would not be opened to him?

The work table was bare of papers, and Ineny stood irresolute. It had been ten minutes since the house servant had shown him in. He wondered if he should sit in his familiar seat, but for some reason it looked less inviting, less safe than it had before. Despite himself he felt like a stranger in the room.

There was nothing odd in Ay's manner when he entered, and Ineny felt reassured.

'Please sit down,' said the old man, motioning to Ineny's chair and taking his own seat. He reached for the jar of wine which stood with beakers on the table and poured it himself. Conscious of the honour, Ineny drew himself up in his seat. He had not deserved such a fate, but his conscience was already encouraging him to think of his act of treachery as an aberration. That was why the gods had made it fail.

'Thank you, lord,' he said, standing to accept the proffered cup. Holding it, he remained standing. Something in Ay's expression held him.

'Drink,' said Ay. 'To my future.'

Ineny continued to stand, holding the cup. In the far recesses of his stomach, his instinct told him to beware; but there was nothing he could do. There was a movement in the room and he shifted his gaze slightly to see that two of Ay's body servants had entered. Ay sat back, looking at him with faintly amused detachment, the corners of his lips curling upwards almost imperceptibly. One of the men came forward and bent over Ay, whispering to him. Ay nodded, pleased. He looked at Ineny indulgently.

'Drink,' he said.

There was no escape. Perhaps it was nothing after all. He raised the beaker, and then, seized with recklessness, drained it.

For a moment nothing happened. He looked at Ay and even registered the change in the old man's expression. In these last moments of his life he realised that Ay knew. But how?

Then a pain came into his head like a bronze chisel, driven into the centre of the forehead and easing it apart. At the same time there was an overpowering revulsion of the stomach, though when he retched nothing but bitter air rose to his mouth. At that moment the light of the rising sun burst into the room, filling it, it seemed to Ineny, with a white brilliance which blotted everything else out; every detail, every person; and which grew greater and greater in power, until it was the only thing in the universe, and he was one with it.

# ELEVEN

'What has happened to your face?'

Ankhsenpaamun was fascinated, but also concerned. Huy rejoiced at this. It meant that she was beginning to see him as her route to survival. If anything happened to him, she would suffer. Her little hand came up to touch the broken cheek. Her fingertips felt cool and kind.

'I was attacked,' replied Huy. He had not yet returned to his house and the intense activity of the past days had worn him out. The fight with Kenamun seemed to have happened weeks ago.

'Attacked?' Immediately, her tone became imperious. Nobody was going to forget who she was, and he had spoken too abruptly, without respect. There was something else: someone had dared to molest one of her people. In her heart, had Huy become one of her family?

'Please do not ask me now,' he said, more humbly. 'I have a favour to beg.'

'Yes?'

He picked his words carefully. 'Now that the great god Amun has decreed that your grandfather should be heir to Nebkheprure Tutankhamun, the burial of the god-king is assured, and we *must* leave the city.'

She looked at him acutely. 'Don't confuse me with your formality. The real reason we must go is because, although Horemheb has lost the Golden Chair for now, he has not given up.'

'Yes, Lady.'

She smiled. 'I thought so. My heart tells me things, now that the king is dead. I begin to live for myself more, and for the pharaoh that I carry.'

'May he sit on the Golden Chair.'

'Or may *she* do so.'

Huy nodded. 'Of course. But it is rare.'

'But it has happened. Makare Hatshepsut was pharaoh in her time.'

'Are we not back to an old contention?'

She smiled again. 'I am content to leave, if I have Ay's assurance that the succession will pass to the child in my birth-cave.'

'I am sure that he will give it. I guarantee it.'

'But can I trust you?'

'Yes,' said Huy, though his heart was hollow. How polluted man's thinking had become, when deceit had to be used to guarantee the safety of the innocent. Trust, duty, hope – these were concepts that man should never have had – he was not up to them.

'My own people tell me Horemheb is angry.'

'Yes?'

'Kenamun is dead. Horemheb thinks Ay's agents did it. Something about a body downriver, which a fisherman noticed as the *matet* boat rose in the sky. But the crocodiles dragged it under.'

'I need your help.'

'Yes?'

'To leave here, we must travel by the river.'

'Of course.'

'I cannot organise a boat alone. We must leave discreetly. Please understand the need for this.' It was beyond Huy to explain why, but he still hoped to leave behind them convincing proof of the queen's death.

He had expected Ankhsenpaamun to be disagreeable; but her mood had changed, and she entered into the conspiracy with enthusiasm.

'You must ask Taheb,' he suggested.

'Why don't you?'

'I cannot.'

'Why not? You knew her well once.'

'Once!'

'Do you think she cannot be trusted?'

'I do not think that. But no approach from me would be fitting.'

'Why not?' repeated the queen.

Huy fought with his pride. But there was a more important reason: Taheb would not argue if the request came from the queen herself. 'Because we do not know each other as we once did. But was she not a friend of the court? I saw her at Nezemmut's wedding to Horemheb.'

The queen considered. 'Where are we going?'

'Firstly, to Napata.'

'That is to the south!'

'They are loyal. There is nothing to the north but greater danger. And you cannot stay here.'

'So you have told me.'

She remained silent for a long time. Then, 'Did you say *ask*?' she said frostily.

'Tell,' suggested Huy, fighting exhaustion.

'Command.'

Huy was silent.

'Taheb will help,' said the queen slyly. 'Why do you think my little intelligence network is the only part of the royal palace that remains even halfway efficient and loyal?' She paused, looking sad. 'But now it is crumbling too. Of course I recognise the need to depart.'

When Huy returned to his house he hardly recognised it. Nothing was missing, but nothing was out of place either. Everything, even the scrolls on the shelves, was meticulously ordered, and the images of Bes and Horus which presided over his central room were free of dust and sand for the first time in years. The yard was swept and the bathroom so tidy and clean it seemed inconceivable that two nights ago it had witnessed a bloody and fatal battle.

He walked through the rooms which he would soon have to leave forever. Into whose keeping could he place this building, whose arms had encircled his battered body and protected it at the end of so many lonely, desperate days? There would be no time. He would lock up and leave, and that would be all. No doubt later some little official would come snuffling round, because the house did not conform to accepted principles of ownership. There would come a time perhaps when the guardians of conformity would control all life.

He found the note hidden carefully under the statue of Bes. A scrap of paper bearing Ay's cartouche. Remaining only long enough to wash, shave, apply fresh make-up, and change, Huy set off again to see the pharaoh-elect.

He noticed that there were twice as many soldiers in Ay's livery on guard, and he recognised several former members of Horemheb's Black Medjays among them; but Ay was expecting him, and he was admitted quickly. The old man received him in a crowded room through which a number of body servants and scribes passed. At two tables, secretaries were issuing written orders. Huy might have expected to see Ineny playing a prominent part in the preparation for Ay's new status, but decided not to ask what had become of him.

Ay looked younger than Huy had ever seen him, and stood erect, like a youth. His hair was freshly dyed, and his skin shone with oil. He wore a blue-and-gold headdress and a full-length cream tunic, with a pleated kilt that reached to below the knee. His sandals were polished leather, with gold fittings in the shape of snakes and scarabs. He was heavily scented with *seshen*, and his make-up was fashionably pale. His heavy collar matched his headdress, and the balancing *mankhet* which hung down his back was of gold, in the shape of the *tjet* amulet.

He was a king already.

'Huy.'

'Lord.'

Ay smiled broadly. 'I have good news for you.'

'What is it?'

'The means to make your scheme succeed. The gods have sent us a gift.'

'What?'

Ay's face became graver. 'Of course what falls happily for us is also a tragedy. But if life has a purpose, so perhaps does death.'

'What has happened?' Huy's eyes prickled. He blinked to rest them, and forced them wide open. He had smudged a crumb of *kohl* on his lower right eyelash, and it blurred the foreground of his vision.

'I have a body for you to bury as the former queen.'

Huy felt energy surge back into him. 'That indeed is a gift. Where is it?'

'On the river. On its way here from the Northern Capital.'

'But who —?'

Ay was solemn. 'It may be better if Ankhsi does not know — it is little Setepenra.'

'What happened?'

Ay spread his hands. 'We do not know exactly. A snakebite, probably. She was in the palace garden when suddenly she cried out and fell. They called doctors immediately, of course. But by the time they arrived it was too late.'

'When did this happen?'

'The message came by carrier pigeon yesterday, soon after the sun had passed his zenith. I have sent a courier north to find out more, but we sent another pigeon back with orders to put the princess's body on a falcon ship and bring it here. My people will meet it some way downriver of the city, and bring it here after dark. I hope now you will learn to trust me, Huy. I think I have repaid my debt to you.'

Huy looked inwards. If Setepenra's death had indeed been an accident, it could not have happened at a better time. The girl was Akhenaten's sixth daughter, two years younger than Ankhsenpaamun, and in face and body very similar to her sister.

'What about your other granddaughter in the Northern Capital?'

Ay looked at him narrowly. 'What reservations do you have now?' He broke off to smile thinly. 'I was wrong to offer you the archives. I should have suggested Kenamun's job; but I think you'd be too good at it for comfort.' He paused to answer an enquiry from one of the order-issuing secretaries, and then drew Huy apart from the throng of people to stand by a large window opening to a view of the great temple of Amun.

'The princess Neferneferura will soon be leaving the Black Land. For a long time I have been in negotiations, through the vizir of the Northern Capital, with King Burraburiash of the Land of the Twin Rivers. An alliance with them now will be a bulwark against the Hittites. Now the princess is going to marry the king's son.'

'So, all Akhenaten's surviving daughters will be accounted for.'

'None of us likes loose ends,' said Ay lightly, and without waiting for an answer, returned to the centre of the room. 'By the way,' he said over his shoulder and indicating one of the secretaries. 'This is Kenna. You will be liaising with him from now on.' The secretary, an intelligent man of thirty, with close-cropped hair, looked up unsmilingly at Huy and nodded an abrupt greeting.

Ay kept his word. He even managed to provide an excuse for Senseneb to leave the doctors' compound and come to the palace without arousing the suspicions of Merinakhte, by summoning her to consult with him about the arrangements for her father's burial, which would take place soon after the king's. As chief physician, he would be buried in a place of honour on the fringes of the valley. The body of the little princess was brought secretly to a ground-floor room of Ay's palace and there Senseneb applied what little make-up and hair dye was

159

necessary to turn the dead girl into her sister's double. Once dressed in a set of the queen's robes, the transformation was complete. Keeping it from Ankhsenpaamun was a problem which the queen solved herself, saying that she did not want to see the body which would be left in her place, or know the identity of its owner. She would offer prayers for the safe passage of its soul to Thoth and Osiris, and to Isis and Nephthys.

'How is your wound?' asked Senseneb, when they were together at his house.

'Sore.'

She smiled, touching it. 'The stitches should stay in three more days, but I think you have healed enough for me to take them out before I leave.' Her voice trailed off as she spoke the last words.

'Have courage.'

She looked at him, taking his hand. 'I am trying. But my heart tells me I will never see you again.'

'I will follow as soon as I am sure Ay is not planning to send anyone after you.'

'He gave his word.'

Huy smiled.

'Has a boat been arranged?'

'A light sailing barge of Taheb's fleet with papyrus from the Delta is taking you. The papyrus will be delivered at Soleb, but the captain has orders to take you on to Napata.'

'Can he be trusted?'

'The boatowner can. She is loyal to the queen. As for the captain, there is gold for him to collect in Napata – for his personal use.'

Senseneb smiled sadly. 'The last thing I shall ever want again when this is over is adventure.'

Huy was silent, then looked at her seriously. 'There is something else.'

'Yes?' The gravity of his voice scared her.

'If, when you get to Napata, for any reason you do not feel safe, you must take the queen with you and travel on to Meroe. No one from the Southern Capital would follow you that far, and there are people in the far south who are still loyal to the line of Akhenaten. They will protect his daughter.'

Sensenseb's head swam. She did not want to go to Meroe. All her big city instincts rose up against it. At least Napata was still recognisably a Black Land town, belonging to the southern part of the empire. Meroe was at its farthest limits. It was further from the Southern Capital than the Great Green was to the north. Privately she made up her mind that the danger would have to be very great to make her retreat so far, and she doubted if Ankhsenpaamun would be eager to go either; but she said nothing. Her heart told her that she was embarking on an adventure so mad that she would regret it for the rest of her life.

'When do we leave?' she asked, knowing that it was too late to back out now.

'Dawn.'

'So soon?'

'Yes.'

'But what about us?'

'There is no time. Princess Setepenra's body will be taken to the royal palace today. The queen will remain there until tonight, when she will board the boat at the southern quay. You must return to your house, tell Hapu, pack what you need, and as soon as it is dark, come back to me here. Today you must behave as if it were any ordinary day.'

'When shall I come tonight?'

'As soon as it is safe.'

She looked at him. 'But if I am not leaving until dawn, how will we pass the time?'

'Sealing the knot,' said Huy, and kissed her.

As the sun passed from his *matet* to his *seqtet* boat, Sensenseb's apprehension gave place to excitement. She had packed a

161

leather satchel with Hapu's help, and found that she needed very little, though she wondered how much the queen would be taking, and decided then that a little more than what she needed would do.

Her *Ka* went on ahead of her, and she began to wonder what the house in Napata would be like. She had not seen it since childhood, and she thought about the couple who had always been its caretakers. She had sent a letter to warn them of her arrival with a friend. They would not recognise the queen. How would they react when they saw her, Senseneb, grown up? What questions about her life would they ask? Would she dare tell them that her husband would be joining them later – or would that be a hopeful lie to tempt the anger of the gods? She came to realise that her only regret was that Huy was not leaving with her. Leaving the Southern Capital, she came to realise, was not a matter of regret at all.

She had just given orders to Hapu about the disposal of her father's little menagerie, which she was certainly not leaving to the mercy of Merinakhte, when the doctor himself arrived. Her heart beat so fast that her chest hurt, her stomach felt hollow and her head flew; but since he appeared to notice nothing she assumed that she had herself under control.

Merinakhte had dressed up. He had rubbed ochre into his cheeks, and lined his eyes with *kohl*. He wore a pleated over-kilt in a lattice pattern, knotted at the side, with a fringed sash and a decorated apron which fell below the knee. His tunic had open, pleated sleeves.

'Where are you going?' she asked.

He smiled ruefully. 'I am glad you've noticed that I made an effort. I'm not going anywhere. I have come to apologise. What I said to you was cruel. I beg your forgiveness and ask you to accept this gift.'

She looked at his grey eyes carefully, but they were without expression. She noticed with alarm that he was looking round the room into which Hapu had led him. Would he see signs of her departure?

'I would have come sooner but your gate has always been locked. Have you been away?'

'No – just busy.'

'Here.' He held out a glass jar, worked in a blue-and-white pattern of interwoven ribbons. Its base and top were chased gold, the base sculpted into waves and the top in the form of a sea-beast, riding more waves and carrying a trumpet-shell. 'It is from Kheftyu. An ointment perfume made of mermaids' milk.'

She must not antagonise him. The jar was heavy. The glass it was made of must be very thick. She lifted the lid, and released a delightful odour.

'Don't use it now,' he said, hurriedly. 'It would be a pity to waste it.'

A faint warning sounded in her heart, but she dismissed it as part of the revulsion he had always engendered in her. And yet now he seemed a new man – perfectly sincere. Was it possible that his divided *Ka* had begun to find a way towards unity?

'Thank you,' was all she said.

To her relief, he turned to go. 'I must be at the House of Healing. I wanted to make my peace with you.'

'You have.'

'Good.' He hesitated. 'My offer stands. The love bond is there for me.'

'I am sorry.'

He bowed his head. 'Well, if you change your mind . . .' He left the sentence hanging. 'There may come a time when you will be glad to.'

# TWELVE

Ay stood alone in his work room, watching the sun go down and dusk gather around the temple of Amun. The high priest would arrange for the god to show his approval of the succession to the people two days later. Soon after that, Ay would be alone in the Southern Capital. Little Ankhsi would be gone, and General Horemheb would be leading five falcon ships and five more regiments to the Delta, where he would take overall command of the northern army. Among the soldiers accompanying him, Ay had placed Kenna and four other men he knew he could trust. Horemheb had agreed to the proposal that he go north with surprising ease, and Ay was not such a fool as to think that he would not take advantage of the army if he could.

But it was better to have him there than intriguing here. The longer the general stayed in the Southern Capital, the more Ay risked having his authority undermined. Once he was out of the way, it would be easier to pursue his diplomatic links with the Land of the Twin Rivers, with Mitanni, and with the peoples to the south of the Black Land. Ay planned to raise an army which would be able to stand against anything Horemheb could throw at him, if their conflict ever pitched the empire into civil war. But he hoped it would not come to that. Perhaps Horemheb would fall under a Hittite spear. Whatever else he was, he was a brave man, and always joined battle at the head of his troops. And if the Hittites could not do it, then an arrow fired by Kenna might do the job. Ay was the last person to deny Horemheb an honourable death and a state funeral, provided he could succeed in sending him to the Fields of Aarru; and a simple assassination would be so much less costly than a civil war.

There was also the question of his succession to be settled. Ay had finally abandoned the idea of ever marrying Ankhsenpaamun – which was why he was letting her go so easily. A daughter of the Great Criminal was not, after all, going to get the unreserved blessing of the powerful priesthood. His thoughts were turning to a princess from one of the lands to the north-east. The world was changing. The Black Land could no longer stand alone and supreme. Survival lay in the realisation of that.

It had grown dark outside, and the heat caressed his face, cocooning him, soothing him. He luxuriated in the quiet that follows victory. He thought about the little boat Taheb had supplied, tied up now at the southern quay. Soon Ankhsi would be embarking, and at dawn, before he had even awoken, perhaps, she would be gone. He had sent men ahead to Napata to watch her, but he doubted if she would trouble him again.

He would keep his promises about the funerals. He regretted that there was not time to give Tutankhamun a magnificent one, for such a thing would unquestionably be to his credit. But his right to perform the Opening of the Mouth was inalienable now. Horaha, too, would be buried according to his dignity. Ay feared the dead. He was too close to them not to.

As for little Setepenra, she, too, would go gloriously to Osiris. There was no doubt that Horemheb would be deceived into thinking that she was the queen: he wanted the queen dead, and he would not look for deceit in something which was to his advantage. Soon after dawn, a body servant would discover her. Kenna would be sent to investigate officially, and Merinakhte would pronounce that she had died of grief for her departed husband.

Ay breathed in the night air appreciatively. It was all perfect.

*     *     *

165

Senseneb was ready. She tried to breathe calmly, but she could not be still. She looked round the house which had been her home for so long for a last time, and brought her father into her heart. She ached, but the thought of what lay ahead did not permit her to dwell on her departure from all that she knew and, foolishly thinking it would never change, had learned to trust.

Hapu would take her to the harbour quarter. When he slung her two bags over his shoulder and opened the door, the night air entered. It was like the life beyond beckoning, and she could not stop her tears.

'Wait.'

She needed an excuse to delay a moment longer. Once she was with Huy, once she was on her way, it would be all right. But it was this moment between home and travel that was hard to bridge. She looked round the room.

She had no intention of taking Merinakhte's gift with her, and had told Hapu to return it to him as soon as she was safely gone; but now she turned to the blue jar on the shelf. Mermaids' milk. Its scent had been beautiful. Perhaps she should put a little on. She wanted to be as attractive as possible for Huy. It would be their last night together for a time whose length she could not guess at. Glancing at Hapu, she crossed the room and picked up the jar. She uncapped it and the delicious odour once again met her nostrils. She placed it on the table and took off her rings.

'There isn't much time,' said Hapu. Tears were in his eyes too.

'I'll hurry.' She would just smooth a little of the cream on her cheeks and neck, she thought, as she put her rings down.

Suddenly one of the two cats that formed part of Horaha's little zoo, a large tabby with a white bib, darted in from outside. He leapt on to the table, and, head and tail held high, walked towards Senseneb, purring. He was distracted by the perfume jar, sniffing at it daintily with his sensitive nose. Then, with a decided movement, he knocked it over. The thick white liquid inside spilled onto the table. The cat leapt to the floor and vanished.

Senseneb had righted the jar before she noticed that the spilt ointment was burning into the wood. She watched it in horror. Her heart would not accept what she saw. She was brought back by Hapu's voice, speaking evenly.

'I'll kill him,' he said. 'Now, you must come.'

Huy thought he must have slept deeply, but not for more than an hour. He was not sure that she had at all. At first, after her arrival, she had been bright, even scintillating, and he thought it was excitement. She had only been grave in saying farewell to Hapu, who would not stay but had taken his leave immediately. Then she had removed the stitches from Huy's face. There had been no pain.

Huy, who lived alone without servants, had prepared a meal of duck and *ful* himself, but they had eaten and drunk frugally. He looked at Senseneb and wondered what she was keeping back from him.

She kept very still, knees drawn up to her chin, looking inwards. Huy had not disturbed her. He wanted to embrace her, comfort her, and add the strength of his heart to hers, but he knew that she did not want to be touched yet. She would tell him when she was ready. Although it was only the third hour of night, the dawn seemed very close, and the threat of it drove quietness of spirit from them both.

'It is worse for the queen,' said Huy, finally. 'She is all alone.'

Senseneb looked at him. Should she tell him what had happened? She had ordered Hapu not to. There was no point in burdening him with it; he had too much to think about and soon she would be safe. She considered Hapu's safety more. Once Merinakhte knew he had been thwarted in his vengeance, where his madness would take him? Or did he really believe that once she was deformed she would accept him?

'I know,' she said finally, softening, and as they embraced

she felt such sweet relief that she wondered at having resisted so long. They did not make love, but this was as great a pleasure as lovemaking, to be wrapped in the happiness of each other's warmth. He buried his nose and lips in her dark hair, felt the fine contour of her head with them, and kissed her gently. They stayed like that for a long time, while outside all sound ceased. Then he must have slept. Later, the dark panel framed by the window began to grow light, so slowly at first that Huy thought it was a trick of his eyes; but a distant bird on the riverbank cried.

'Come,' said Huy.

Dawn is a sad time for parting, he thought, as he picked up Senseneb's bags and followed her into the silent street. He wondered if there was ever a good time; but the worst was dawn.

They set out on foot and in silence for the southern quay. The only sound was their sandals on the earth. Each felt they should have a multitude of things to say; but neither had a word. It was a relief when they saw the yellow lantern on the boat ahead. A shadow detached itself from the harbour wall and came to meet them, resolving itself into a man.

'We must leave at once,' said the captain. 'The queen and her body servants are aboard.' He turned to Huy. 'Lady Taheb is accompanying us.'

'Does she know I am here?'

'No.'

'I will see her when the time does not press.'

The captain nodded.

Huy took Senseneb's hand.

She looked at him. 'You think you have all the time in the world, and suddenly it is gone. Goodbye.'

'Goodbye. Do not linger. I will come to you soon.'

She was crying silently. 'There is so much danger. Do not die.'

'No.'

'I long for you.'

'I long for you.'

Huy watched her follow the captain up the gangplank to the dark boat which rocked in the red flood water of the River. She did not look back. He watched them cast off, and watched as the wind caught the hoisted sail and drew the sleek ship out into the stream. The River was broad like a sea. He stood there until the boat was just a speck on it.

'A touching sight,' said a voice dry as sand and as lonely as the desert behind him. Huy turned to see Merinakhte's gaunt figure leaning against the corner of a shed. It was almost light now, but there were no other ships drawn up at the southern quay, and they were alone. Merinakhte's shadow reached from where he stood to the edge of the water.

'She didn't use the ointment I sent her to pretty herself up for you.' The voice carried a detached regret.

'I don't understand you,' said Huy. The doctor was dressed in rather battered finery, and the ochre and *kohl* on his face had rubbed and run. He looked tired but his eyes were hard.

'Then perhaps you will understand this!'

The jolt into screaming rage caught Huy off guard, but even for a man of his speed and length of stride, Merinakhte had too great a distance to cover to make his first attack pay, and the bronze surgical scalpels he held in each hand stabbed air. He wheeled round instantly, gulping air, but there was fear in his face now, along with the fury. Unless he killed Huy cleanly and quickly, he had thrown his entire career away by this one action. That was as far as his thoughts ran. He had bidden sanity farewell long ago, and sacrificed ambition to vengeance. Blood swam before his eyes as they focused on his prey. He raised his stabbing arms again, his hands like claws around the hafts of the knives. Huy had turned too, using the two or three seconds before Merinakhte resumed his attack to look desperately around him for a weapon. The quay was bare. There was not even a wooden spar on the ground. If he used his own knife, he would have to close with the doctor, and he did not relish the idea. But he reached behind him and drew it from its sheath at the back of his belt.

The sight of a weapon drawn against him checked Merinakhte's onslaught and he dropped his arms, hissing. He crouched, circling Huy, looking for an opportunity to dart in and stab before his opponent had a chance to use his knife. Huy backed away. He was between Merinakhte and the water now. The current, even this close to shore, was very fast. Only the strongest swimmer could avoid being swept away.

Then he noticed the rope. It was a heavy ship's line loosely coiled by the bronze ring to which it was attached. He looked quickly to see if Merinakhte had seen it too, but the doctor's eyes were fixed on him. Gradually, Huy retreated until he was within reach of the rope. Then he dropped to one knee.

'Don't kill me,' he pleaded.

With a shriek of triumph Merinahkte charged. Huy seized the rope and flung it towards him. It snaked between his legs and tripped him. He fell forwards heavily, the blades of the scalpels snapping as they hit the quay. Merinakhte had hit the ground heavily, and Huy saw blood burst in the centre of his face as his nose was crushed. He moved in quickly, but Merinakhte was staggering to his feet.

The only thought in Huy's heart was to kill him; he saw himself seize the man by one wrist and the waistband of his kilt, and hurl him into the river.

But there had been too many deaths. Huy paused. Before Merinakhte could recover he had placed his thumbs behind the doctor's ears and pressed until the man passed out. Ay's justice would be harsher than drowning; but Huy was too much of a coward to take another life. He heard shouts, and, looking up, saw three scared young longshoremen approaching. On the ground, a pool of urine spread from Merinakhte's loins.

Ay took the Golden Chair in the last days of the season of *akhet,* so that the people would be free to farm as soon as possible after the end of the flood. It coincided with news from the north of great victories by Horemheb over the Hittites, giving the Blacklanders a second reason to rejoice, for the conscripted soldiers would soon be coming home. Horemheb had sent word that there was nothing now that could not be dealt with by regulars.

The High Priest of Amun made much of the good news, coming as it did on the back of the magnificent funerals of Tutankhamun and his queen, for which Ay had revived many more of the old rituals suppressed during the days of the Great Criminal. The priests acclaimed Ay as the bringer of peace and stability to the Black Land at last, and all the portents were that he would live happily and long. The popularity that ten days' celebration at his expense had brought him was undeniable, and the drinking house talk was of a new marriage, an heir, and a new dynasty, founded on peace as fully as the last had been on war.

'I never thought I would see this house again,' said Senseneb, looking round the cramped living room into which the sun shone, making the spiralling dust sparkle.

'I never thought we would see the Southern Capital again,' replied Huy, looking at his old home with the eyes of a stranger. Had it only been eighty days since he had left it? And yet even the journey back from Meroe, where they had left the queen in the care of the governor, seemed like a dream.

'Do you regret leaving here?'

Huy could not answer the question. It was too soon to tell. But he could not disappoint the hope in her voice. In a very short time, Senseneb had taken to life in the country; and he still believed in the love bond between them.

'No,' he replied at last. 'But it is good to return, and to see that Ay kept his word.'

'Yes. My father's *Ka* will be at peace.'

'Will you go to the doctors' compound?'

She shook her head. 'I will see Hapu, but I will not revisit

171

my past. I would be like a ghost returning to a place which everyone it knew has left.'

They fell silent. Huy thought of Merinakhte. Ay had ordered him to be impaled, and Huy had seen the execution. He had bribed the impalers to give the young doctor flame liquor before they killed him. It was an act of mercy he owed his enemy, for he knew that he should have given Merinakhte to the River at the end of their fight. But Merinakhte had refused to drink, twisting his head and lips away from the proffered bottle so violently that in the end the executioners had given up. It had been a bad death.

Huy looked around the room again, to clear his heart, recognising his old possessions – the statues of Horus and Bes, the battered furniture, the papyrus scrolls in their niche. They seemed to belong to someone else now. Perhaps, in a way, they did.

'What will you do with this house?' asked Senseneb.

Huy had asked himself that question. The answer depended upon many things. He had the chance of a new life in the south, but something made him reluctant to let go of the old. Was it just natural caution? He would return to Napata now. That was certain. Perhaps there an answer would come to him. It did not matter how long it took, there was no hurry. Ay had even told him he could practise as a scribe again. But now that it was possible at last, discontent stirred in a corner of his heart. He looked inwards at a picture of himself: a provincial scribe, living out his life by the river under the southern sun. It was a restful, calm, uneventful picture.

'Ipuky, the Master of the Silver Mines, gave me this house. I will talk to him about what to do.'

'Why do you need someone else's advice?'

Huy took her hands, but he knew what the house meant to him. Still, he would not deny himself this chance of happiness. Happiness. Another word with no certain meaning. Another idea which constantly slipped around the next corner ahead of you. What had made him like this? Should he ask her to exchange vows when he still had such doubts? She was expecting him to.

He looked at her eyes, caught in the sunlight. Ra in his splendour visiting even this little corner of his world. From the harbour, they could hear a band, and cheering. The festivities were in their last day. The royal barge would soon be leaving with its escort for the new god-king's state visit to the Northern Capital.

'Will Kheperkheprure Ay be the father of a dynasty of peace?' said Senseneb. Her voice showed her concern at the silence between them.

'I do not know,' said Huy.

They stood together, foreheads touching, their hands on each others' shoulders, neither caring, after all, about Ay's reign, or Horemheb's victories, or anything else at all, in the world or in the future, except their own destiny.

Huy drew in his breath to ask her the question.

## A NOTE ON THE AUTHOR

Anton Gill was born in Essex, and spent part of his early life in
Bamberg, Franconia. He was educated at Chigwell School and
Clare College, Cambridge, and later worked for the English
Stage Company, the Arts Council, the BBC and TV-AM. *City
of the Dead* is his third novel.